I0534843

Feathers and Fatalities

A Vampire Veterinary Mystery

Book 1

Sedona Jade

With Amy Stake & Sedona Ashe

Copyright © 2024 by Gobble Ink, LLC

www.authorsedonaashe.com

Cover and interior artwork by Cauldron Press

www.cauldronpress.ca

A huge thank you to-

Allison Woerner for Alpha Reading.

Maxine Meyer for Copy Editing.

Imogen Evans for Proofreading & Editing.

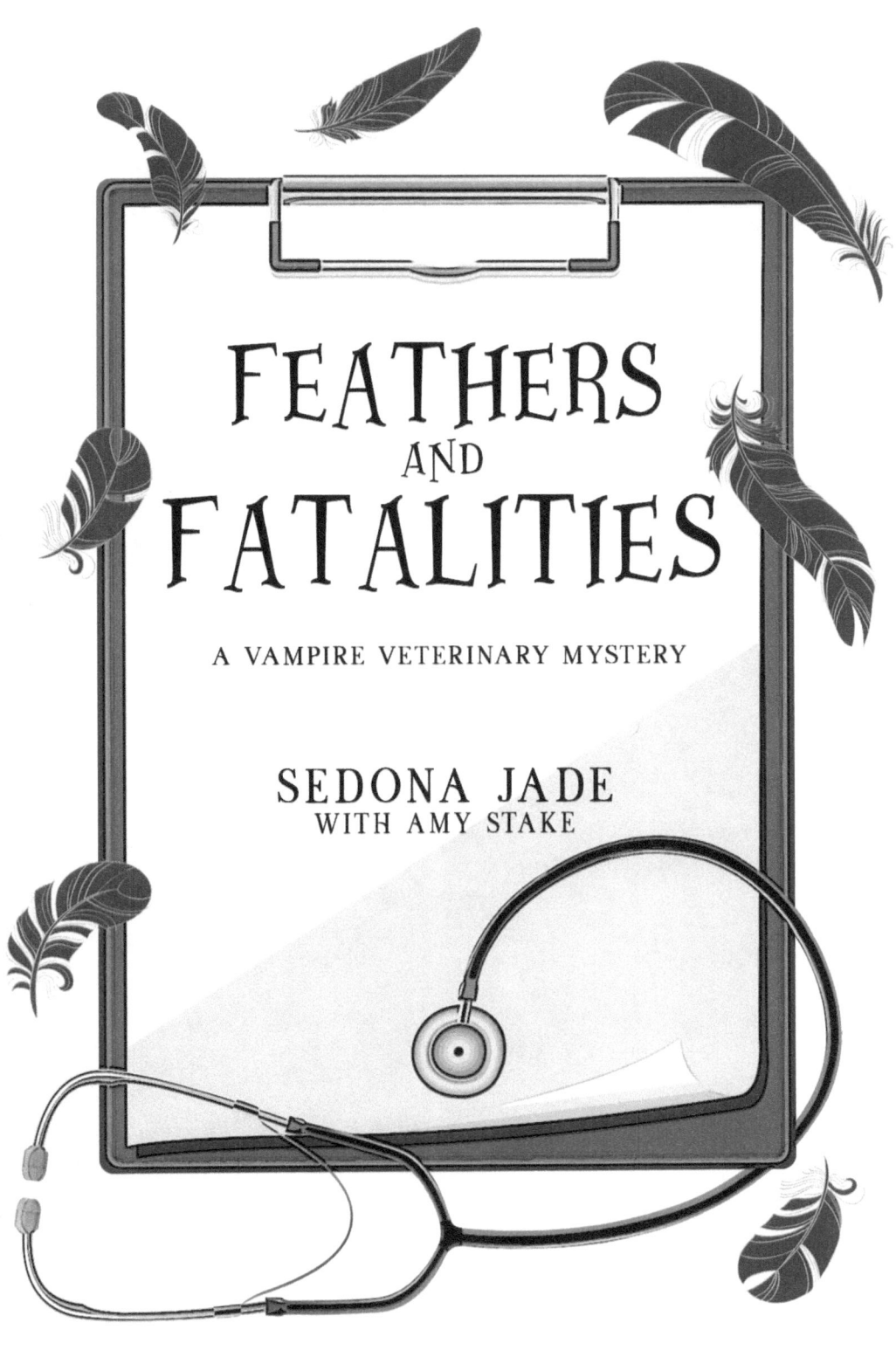

FEATHERS
AND
FATALITIES

A VAMPIRE VETERINARY MYSTERY

SEDONA JADE
WITH AMY STAKE

CONTENTS

CHAPTER ONE

I f you ever find yourself locked in a room with a werewolf mid-shift, don't run. The best thing you can do, other than roll yourself into a tiny pretzel and pray your yoga classes will finally pay off, is play dead. In my case, it helped tremendously to actually be dead, which was why I was still breathing.

Crouching under the operating table, I used one hand for balance while digging around my lab coat pocket for a sedative. Above me, the wolf in question snarled, sending warm doggie spit dripping down the leg of the table to land on the toe of my shoe.

I rolled my eyes, wiping the slobber off with the back of my sleeve. Sometimes, being a veterinarian in a town overrun with paranormal creatures wasn't the glamorous position I envisioned it to be. There were days that even someone like me, a pure-blooded vampire with eight years of vet school, couldn't get through easily.

Today was one of those days.

Everything had been going great until Clark Sommers had shoved his cousin inside the back door and high-tailed it out of there. One look at the kid and I knew we were about to have a problem on our hands. It turned out I was correct.

Clark's cousin was a junior werewolf who hadn't gotten a grip on how to control the shift, and it was a miracle I managed to get him into the back before the human patients could witness his shift—which was how I ended up in a room with an angry werewolf who couldn't turn back to his human form.

Ah, there was nothing like helping people, only to have it come back and bite me in the behind. I jumped as sharp canines snapped above my head, reminding me I needed to hurry before I ended up with more than a metaphorical bite.

A loud knock reverberated through the operating room, causing the wolf to growl.

"Everything all right in there, Ophelia?" a voice sounded on the other side of the door.

"All good!" I yelled out, even though nothing was actually going great. "Can you help Bree in the front? I'll be out shortly!"

I listened carefully as the footsteps retreated, my shoulders sagging in relief. Justin Case, one of the clinic's vet techs, was very capable at his job, but he enjoyed sticking his nose where it didn't belong. Normally, I would have welcomed assistance with a disgruntled patient, but there was one small problem with letting Justin into the room.

He was human. And just like most of the human residents of Bluejay Falls, he was in the dark when it came to the existence of all things supernatural. If it went bump in the night, it remained a mystery. Paranormal species were regarded as bedtime stories told to entertain children and not the very real creatures we were.

I couldn't blame humans. Those of us with special abilities could be a danger to the people around us without intending to cause harm. *Bloody Mary!* If I could close my eyes and pretend I wasn't about to get mauled by an angry teen wolf with raging hormones and an attitude, I'd do it in a heartbeat.

The table shook, and for a moment, I thought the legs might snap under the wolf's weight as he leaped from the table to the floor. Less than a heartbeat later, I found myself staring directly at the sharp teeth he'd been snapping above my head.

The wolf snarled again, his head tilting to the side to inspect me. As slowly as I could manage, I raised my free hand palm out and held it an inch from his wet, gaping mouth.

"Easy there," I whispered between clenched teeth.

As scary as they appeared, more often than not, if you used a calm voice with a werewolf, they tended to back down. All those stories people told about being hunted by those beautiful creatures were nothing but lies made to scare children into obeying their parents and not straying too far into the woods alone.

In reality, werewolves were fairly docile, and it wasn't too hard to coax them into snuggles and belly rubs. Which is why, out of all the supernaturals around, they were by far my favorite.

The wolf let out a monstrous howl, revealing his canines as he readied to pounce on me.

I blew out a sigh. Clearly, there were exceptions to every rule.

"That's how you want to play this?" I asked. "Fine. But don't say I didn't warn you!"

Before the wolf could make his move, I vamped out. My eyes, usually a pale green, turned blood red, and my pupils narrowed to thin slits as vampire strength flowed through my body. Pushing my locks of long, red curls from my face revealed the dark veins of poison that spread like spider-webs beneath my skin.

One hiss was all it took for the wolf to take a step back.

The wolf whined, realizing his mistake in a hurry.

"That's right, buddy. You're not the alpha here."

As he clambered away from me, I leaped forward, wrapping my arms around him and tackling him to the ground. The wolf tried to get out from under me, but I didn't give him a chance. Sitting astride his back, I pushed aside the plush fur on his right thigh and jabbed the needle filled with sedative into the fat.

He yelped and tried his best to scramble out from beneath me, but I held tight, petting between his ears as his muscles relaxed and he dozed off. When I was certain he had entered a deep sleep, I stood and dusted off my coat. A cloud of wolf fur floated in the air and covered the floor. People who talked about how much huskies shed had never cuddled a werewolf.

Opening a cabinet, I pulled out a clean sheet to drape over the sleeping werewolf. Unfortunately, clothes didn't make the shift, and I'd helped enough wolves to know he would shift forms before waking. The last thing I needed was a naked man walking out of the room and through the clinic. After draping the sheet over him, I realized how thin the sheet was and decided to grab a second sheet to layer on him—just to be sure no one who happened to be in the clinic when he awakened got an eyeful.

Wiping my brow, I stepped out into the hallway and locked the door behind me. Glancing at the gold watch on my hand—a graduation present from Mom and Dad years ago—I straightened and walked toward the front of the clinic for my next appointment.

"Hey, boss. How's the furball doing?" Bree asked.

My eyes traveled over the pixie, and I smiled at her outfit choice for the day. Bree, my other vet tech, was the exact opposite of Justin. And not just because she was a paranormal. Where Justin was professional and constantly overdressed, Bree showed up to work in a state of perfect chaos.

Today, her pink hair was tied haphazardly in a top knot. Neon-colored pens had been jammed into her hair, and I suspected she'd forgotten they were there. Under her lab coat, she wore a rainbow-colored jumpsuit that reached past her ankles, and I spotted glittery rubber clogs peeking out from the hems. The glitter was an exact match to the one she dusted over her lids.

To put it bluntly, Bree looked like a rainbow had farted on her, or she was doing her best impersonation of a disco ball. Either way, it was completely on-brand for a pixie. They were a flashy species that loved color and anything that sparkled.

Grinning, I picked up the stack of file folders at the front desk. "He'll be fine once he sleeps it off. Did Justin suspect anything?"

"Clueless as ever," she replied with a smirk.

As my clinic grew and more paranormal patients found their way to my practice, it was becoming harder to keep Justin from finding out. But he was a wonderful tech, and I didn't want to let him go either.

I thumbed through the folders, noting the patient names. Peering out of the sliding glass in the office wall that gave me a view of the waiting area out front, I took in the lineup for the evening. Instantly, I recognized some of our regulars.

Double-checking the files, I glanced at Bree. "Mrs. Claude is back again?"

The pixie nodded.

I pinched the bridge of my nose, unsure I wanted to ask, but doing it anyway. "What is it this time?"

"She thinks Vincent ate her car keys." Bree giggled.

My lips formed a tight line as I fought the urge to laugh

or groan in frustration. "She thinks the snake ate her keys? Really?"

"If you ask me, she probably lost them! Remember the time she thought he ate her diamond earrings, but they turned up in the shower?"

"I do, and you're probably right," I told Bree. "I take it Justin is handling Dusty's vaccines?"

"Uh-huh. He should be done soon. Which patient do you want me to assign to him next?"

Trailing over the names on the list, I picked out two I knew wouldn't be tough to handle and gave their files to Bree.

Sunny Days Veterinary Clinic was the only vet clinic in town open from dusk till dawn. Despite being a born vampire who could go out in the sunlight with no issues, I chose the odd schedule to accommodate the paranormal creatures that might not have the benefit of being out during the day. I was an emergency vet for regular pets and a specialty service for those who weren't exactly normal. It was a win-win in my books.

Unfortunately, the late-night hours made finding good techs a constant battle. That was why, when Justin and Bree showed up with their résumés one week apart, and neither had minded working nights, I'd hired them both on the spot. Blood-sucking beggars couldn't be choosers.

My stomach growled on cue, and I winced when Bree's lavender eyes darted to it.

"I'll be right back." I set the folders down on the desk and ducked into the small kitchenette off the main hallway.

My fingers locked around the door of the mini fridge, and I looked over my shoulder to make sure the coast was clear before sliding open the secret compartment in the back. Licking my lips, I reached in to pull out a juice box of Crimson Quench.

While vamps still needed blood to survive, no one said it had to come from a human or be consumed in a grotesque fashion. To put it bluntly, biting was antiquated, and blood juice boxes were the way of the future.

Lips locking around the multicolored straw, I was halfway through the drink when a low chittering caught my attention. Looking up at the corner of the room, I stared at the tiny bat hanging off the ceiling-mounted television. "Hi, Byrd. I wondered where you'd been hiding all day."

The little guy glared at me with narrowed eyes, then draped a wing over his face.

"Rude!" Ignoring the snarky bat, I reached for the remote and turned the TV on.

This wasn't the first time Byrd had acted like a jerk, nor would it be the last. For someone who got to live at the clinic rent-free, you'd think he'd be a little nicer. Instead, he behaved as though he owned the place. He was lucky he was so darn cute, otherwise I wouldn't put up with it.

The television flickered to life, and a picture of the news station appeared on the screen. Lowering the volume, I watched the captions at the bottom as I finished my liquid lunch.

Behind me, the door swung open. "Another robbery?"

Justin asked as he waltzed in, heading straight for the coffee machine.

"It seems so," I answered, quickly tossing the empty juice box into the trash and dropping a crumpled-up paper towel on top before he could see it.

The label was discreet, and he'd likely just think it was cherry juice, but I preferred not answering questions.

Justin pressed a button, tapping his foot while waiting for the machine to work its magic. "This town is going down the drain fast."

I grimaced. "I'm sure they'll catch whoever is responsible soon. Bluejay Falls is one of the safest places to live in the country."

"Right," Justin said, his disbelief palpable.

He reached into his coat pocket and pulled out a stick of wasabi-flavored gum, tossing it into his mouth. One time, I'd tried to count how many of those he ate in a day and lost track after reaching the double-digits. The man really loved his gum.

Justin raked his fingers through his over-gelled black hair. "Bree said you're taking the python and the two new clients?"

I nodded.

"Cool. Mind if I skip out a little early tonight?"

Tilting my head, I inspected the crisp shirt Justin wore under his lab coat and the polished, pointed-toe dress shoes poking out from the hem of his gray slacks. I sniffed, breathing in the scent of cloves and pine, Justin's signature cologne.

I folded my arms over my chest and smirked. "Big date?"

"Something like that," he answered, his blue eyes sliding away from mine. "Is that a problem?"

Shaking my head, I widened my grin. "Not at all. Have fun!"

Not bothering to reply, Justin took his coffee mug and shot one last glance at the television before leaving me alone in the kitchen. The smell of his cologne lingered in the air long after he was gone, and I wondered who it was Justin had plans with. I still knew very little about him despite having been his boss for over five months. Unlike Bree, Justin kept his private life to himself, and I respected that about him.

It was one thing we had in common.

Checking the doggie-shaped clock on the wall, I squared my shoulders and turned off the television. My gaze flicked to the sleeping bat underneath, and I chuckled under my breath as I opened the door to leave. Five more hours before I could head home. With any luck, I could go the rest of the night without another paranormal incident.

I saluted the bat and backed out of the room. "Enjoy your nap, Byrd."

CHAPTER TWO

A s the clock ticked away, the evening rush continued into the night. Soon, the waiting room was buzzing with anxious pet owners and their furry—and not-so-furry—companions.

I greeted each new patient with a smile, trying to soothe their nerves while attending to their pets' needs. From emergencies to routine vaccinations, the night was filled with a steady stream of appointments.

One particularly memorable case involved a frantic call about a potential rabies scare. Rushing to examine the concerned pet, I quickly realized it was a false alarm because of a bottle of expensive conditioner and a frothing mouth. After reassuring the nose-blind and panicking owner and calming down their perfectly healthy but conditioner-covered poodle, I couldn't help but chuckle at the absurdity of the situation.

As the night wore on, fatigue began to set in. Despite my best efforts to stay energized and my love for my patients, the constant demands of the clinic took its toll. My shoulders sagged with exhaustion as I glanced at the clock, longing for the end of the day.

Finally, as the sun reared its head on the horizon, casting a warm glow through the clinic windows, I heaved a sigh of relief. Another night shift at the clinic had come to an end. Taking a moment to collect myself, I savored the quiet stillness of the empty waiting room before tidying up for the night and preparing to head home.

"Thanks for helping with the walk-ins, Bree," I said as the vet tech got ready to leave. "I didn't think we'd get this many patients tonight, or else I wouldn't have agreed to let Justin head out early."

"Anytime. Did he say who his date was with?"

"Not a word," I said with a shrug.

The pixie reached for a long turquoise coat from the closet, slipping it on, and tying it around her waist. Her slender frame, boxed in by the heavy fabric, somehow made her appear even smaller. Pixies were naturally on the short side, but Bree took the cake, and I wondered if her clothes were specially made to fit her miniature size.

"Shocker. Anyway, if you hear anything, text me immediately." Bree wiggled her brows at me with so much force I worried they might leap off her face and land on mine. "Justin hasn't gone out in, well, ever! I'm dying to know who he's going out with!"

With that, the pixie twirled on her heels and walked out.

The rising sun cast her in its golden glow, somehow making Bree appear even more magical. I half-expected her wings to pop out as she trailed off down the street. I was almost disappointed when they remained hidden, even though there was little chance of her slipping up.

Pixies kept their wings locked up tight after an incident on a cruise several years ago. I never learned all the details, but it had caused quite a commotion in the paranormal community. After the cruise, everyone who had magic had been warned to be on high alert, myself included.

Though, in my defense, I'd been careful to hide who I was my entire life.

People didn't take as well to vampire fangs as they did to glittering wings. Probably because one was the stuff of horror films, while the other was straight out of a fairytale —and not the original, dark stories.

Finishing up the last of my paperwork, I locked the clinic behind me. My eyes crinkled as I made my way down Orfus Road toward my car, the onset of the coming cold months sitting low in the air. I flipped up the collar of my leather jacket to keep the wind at bay as I marched toward my parked car two blocks away. As a vampire, my temperature usually ran on the lower end, but the chill of the street made me feel like I was, quite literally, undead.

Shuddering, I sped up my pace.

My thoughts were running a mile a minute as I cataloged all the chores I had to slog through when I got home. In my distraction, I didn't notice the giant sign announcing a clothing shop's blowout sale that stood in my path. My vampire instincts kicked in at the sign of danger, blaring an alarm in my head.

Goosebumps spread over my arms, and I jumped on instinct, clearing the top of the sign by mere inches.

"Oh, my!" a voice yelped behind me. "Are you all right, dear?"

Calming my erratic breathing, I turned around to face Mrs. Stouffville, the proud owner of the bakery. Her naturally gray hair was braided loosely to the side, and the gold-rimmed glasses she always wore slid down her long nose as she inspected me.

I noticed she held a paper bag with the logo for Honeybee Bakery stamped on the front. Mrs. Stouffville opened her shop at around the same time I left work every day and had taken it upon herself to be my personal scone supplier since the first day I opened the doors of the clinic.

I didn't have the heart to tell her I couldn't eat anything human and had been going along with the charade for years. While I couldn't enjoy the bakery treats, I appreciated her kindness.

As expected, she extended her hand, pushing the bag my way. "That's quite the jump you have there, dear."

"Um, right? I was a pole vaulter in high school," I lied, my cheeks burning. *Seriously? A pole vaulter?* "Are you ready to start the day?"

The bakery owner shook her head. "Not even close. I asked my nephew to install security cameras over the weekend"—she pointed to the obnoxious white box above our heads—"and for the life of me, I cannot figure out how to work the thing. You wouldn't know anything about it, would you?"

"I'm not great with technology," I admitted.

Unfortunately, this was true. When I'd hired Bree, she'd made it her personal goal to bring the clinic into the modern century—her words, not mine. Until she'd come along, I was still using analog filing systems for all the patients. "Did your nephew leave instructions?"

The elderly woman held up a stack of papers thicker than the epic fantasies I enjoyed reading on my days off. "What am I supposed to do with these? I swear, I have half a mind to get him over here and take it all down. If it wasn't for..."

She suddenly looked both ways down the street as though she expected someone to arrest us for speaking. When she leaned in closer, I followed suit, feeling instantly foolish.

"I've been a little worried about safety," she whispered. "With all the robberies."

Our heads were so close we almost knocked our foreheads together, and I didn't know why Mrs. Stouffville was whispering like we were plotting a robbery ourselves. When she glanced away, I took the chance to pull back.

That was the thing about a town as small as Bluejay Falls. When exciting things happened around here, everyone knew about it. It didn't help that the town hadn't had so much as a whiff of crime since the eighties, which was the main reason I'd moved here.

After spending most of my younger years living in the

city, I'd needed a change. Though I had to admit, being surrounded by other paranormals had also been a big draw for me as well. Bluejay Falls was known for being the self-established epicenter for all things magic, and it made it easier for a born vamp like me to fit in.

Which was why I'd packed my bags, quit my high-paying veterinary job, and moved here nearly a decade ago. Still, Mrs. Stouffville had a point; the robbery streak was a tad worrisome.

"I'm sure it's nothing to lose sleep over," I told the bakery owner.

Was I trying to convince her or myself?

"Say that to all those businesses that got taken. Why someone would do that in our little town, I'll never know." She glanced behind her, then to the stack of instructions in her hands. "Well, I better get to it. Make sure you warm that scone up when you get home. And tell Marty he owes me a poker rematch!"

Waving goodbye, she headed back into the bakery, letting the door close behind her. I stood in front of the shop for a few moments, my fingers white-knuckling the bag as dread filled my soul. Mrs. Stouffville's words had just reminded me I'd forgotten to call Mom and Dad yesterday, and if I knew my parents, there'd be heck to pay for it later.

Marty and Selina Pane did not do well with missed phone calls. Especially not from their one and only daughter.

Fishing my phone from my purse, I double-checked the time in Florida. My parents' photo popped up on the screen, and I smiled at their ridiculous outfits. Ever since the two ancient vamps retired to live a life on the beach, they'd somehow managed to become the epitome of corny.

As in, matching flower-print jogging suits, obnoxiously loud polo shirts, and oversized sunglasses type of corny. With a smile on my face, I clicked the home button and dropped the phone back in my purse.

Despite their cheerful grins and fashion sense that would make a pixie proud, there was only one thing worse than a worried parent, and that was a worried vampire parent. Seriously, they were a controlling bunch.

Better call them later when I get home.

Picking up the pace, I rushed down the street toward my car and turned the heat on full blast as soon as I settled into the driver's seat. I pulled out of the parking lot and headed toward the small bungalow I'd bought with the last of my savings. It was only a ten-minute ride from the clinic, and I looked forward to starting a new book.

I was already picturing myself snuggled up under a blanket with a box of Crimson Quench and my favorite fuzzy socks on my always-cold feet. Pulling into the driveway, I put the car in park and reached for my purse.

I couldn't stop my chuckling when I spotted the two black ears sticking out of the corner. I opened the top flap and peeked into the bag, already knowing what I would find.

"Hey, Byrd," I told the winged creature hiding inside. "Hitching a ride again?"

The little fella scrunched his nose, his wings curling

around himself as he returned to his snooze. This wasn't the first time I'd come home with the bat in my bag, so I wasn't surprised.

The first time he'd hitched a ride in my bag, I'd jumped three feet out of shock when I'd opened it to find him sleeping inside. Since then, it had become our thing. I'd finish a shift, Byrd would ninja himself into my purse, and we'd ride off into the sunrise together. I wasn't sure why the tiny bat seemed to enjoy following me around, but if I was honest, I was grateful for the company.

Careful not to disturb Byrd, I gently picked up my bag and made my way to the front door. My eyes drifted around my yard, noting the overgrown lawn and the scraggly bushes lining the walkway leading to the house. I'd been so busy running the clinic I'd neglected the upkeep of my house.

If my mom were there, she'd talk my ear off about how a woman's front yard was an indication of her mental state. I didn't know where she got her over-the-top notions, but in my case, she may have been on to something. As I stepped onto the porch, I grimaced at the peeling paint and the dried greenery in the window boxes.

Yep. This place had all the charm of a cranky kraken.

Making a mental note to hire someone who could handle landscaping and paint touch-ups, I opened the front door and slipped inside. The spicy scent of cinnamon candles wafted toward me as I draped my coat on the rack at the entrance. My shoulders sagged in relief.

Home sweet home.

Laying my bag down on the small wooden bench nearby, I stroked Byrd's head with the tip of my finger. "We're home, buddy."

The bat yawned. Stretching his leathery wings, he took flight, disappearing into the belly of the house in seconds. I followed his trajectory as he darted past the small open-concept kitchen, through the living area opposite it, and turned down the narrow hall that led to the bedrooms and bathroom.

There was a scratching sound followed by an eerie silence, and I smiled. Byrd had found his favorite napping spot—the laundry basket.

Still grinning, I kicked off my shoes and headed straight for the fridge. Polishing off a blood box in record time, I took out a second one and stabbed a straw through the top. Closing the fridge door, I headed into the living room. The moment my butt hit the couch, I melted into the dark green fabric with a contented sigh.

Ready for a little me time, I opened my newest fantasy book, but I'd barely read half a chapter before my phone buzzed. Annoyed, I tried to ignore it, but the stupid thing vibrated so hard it caused my bag to topple off the bench, sending the contents clattering across the floor. Groaning loudly, I pushed myself off the couch and walked to pick it up.

The number on the screen was not one I recognized, and I was about to send it to voicemail when I remembered Bree had mentioned routing the clinic calls to my cell phone. It was a test to see how many people required assistance during regular hours. I'd been considering hiring a vet to work during the day so the clinic could stay open around the clock, but I needed to test the waters first by offering emergency services during our closed hours.

Brushing a few curls behind my ear, I straightened my spine and answered. "Sunny Days Clinic, Doctor Ophelia Pane speaking."

Static hissed on the other end of the line.

"Hello?"

"Hi, hello? Is this the veterinary clinic?" a garbled voice asked. "Do I have the right number?"

I checked the screen to see if I had a decent signal. Full bars. Scratching my head, I pressed the phone close to my ear and said, "That's us. How can I help you today?"

"Oh, thank goodness! You have to help me. My parrot— something is wrong with him."

The sensation of my stomach twisting itself into knots was all too familiar. As a veterinarian, I'd encountered countless situations where pet owners were worried about their companions. However, more often than not, their concerns stemmed from minor issues—perhaps their pet ingested human food or exhibited an unfamiliar or quirky behavior.

Experience had taught me that in the majority of these cases, the situation resolved itself, and the animals bounced back to their usual selves... sometimes by the time they arrived at the clinic. But just because it was likely everything would be fine or didn't need immediate emergency vet attention, there was always the chance something serious was going on.

The well-being of the animals under my care was my main priority, so I refused to take any risks with their lives. Each concern voiced by a pet owner warranted thorough investigation and attention. After all, pet owners saw their four-legged family members every day, so they usually knew when something didn't seem quite right. The health of their furry loved ones depended on it.

"Please! Can someone help me? I'm right outside the clinic door, but it's locked."

I frowned. "We're usually not open during the day. Did you say you're outside?"

"Yes," the woman screeched into the phone. "Is there someone who can come check Elvis out? I'm really worried."

With a quick glance at the time, I bit down on the inside of my cheek. If I left now, I could be back in time to get a few hours of sleep in before the evening shift started. My belly rumbled, and the insatiable hunger I often battled after a long night came back to haunt me. I really needed some downtime to recharge my body, but I couldn't say no to a patient in need either.

Squeezing my eyelids shut, I tilted my head back, letting it rest on the wall behind me. "I'll be there in ten minutes. Don't go anywhere."

CHAPTER THREE

B y the time I arrived at the clinic, the owner of the distressed parrot appeared to be in a full-blown meltdown, and I was surprised she hadn't already broken into the clinic. Her purse was overturned on the front stoop and she clutched the bird's travel cage close to her chest as she pressed her nose to the glass door. I wasn't sure what she was trying to see since the clinic's lights were off and it was dark inside, but from where I stood, it looked like she was attempting to melt through the door like a ghost.

"Hello?" I called out as I approached.

"Hello, hello, hello!" the parrot squawked from inside his cage.

Nearing the pair, I fished for the keys in my bag. The parrot's owner spun around, raking her fingers through unruly blonde hair and giving me a once over.

I followed her gaze as she took in my leather jacket and ripped jeans. It wasn't exactly a fashion choice that said, "Trust me with your most precious cargo."

I hoped the woman would remember I wasn't supposed to be working right now.

Her hazel eyes narrowed with concern as they fixated on the dried crimson stain on the fabric of my sleeve. With a subtle flick of my wrist, I tucked the stained sleeve behind my back and hurried to open the front door before the woman could ask questions.

Gesturing with a welcoming sweep of my hand, I urged the woman to step across the threshold and make herself comfortable in the clinic. Meanwhile, my mind raced with thoughts of the necessary tasks waiting for me inside. There was a never-ending loop of things that came with owning your own business, but I tried to shrug them off for the time being and focus on my patient.

Moving as fast as possible, I pulled on a fresh white lab coat and turned my attention to the woman in the waiting room. I crouched down to peer into the cage that housed our avian patient, a stunning Scarlet Macaw. Its feathers, of iridescent reds, blues, and bright yellows, shimmered in the subdued light of the overhead lamps.

Perched on a wooden roost, Elvis tilted his head and watched me with a mixture of curiosity and defiance, his eyes dilating as he followed my every move. This one was a troublemaker, I could feel it. With a sudden ruffle of his feathers and a bob of his head, the bird abruptly turned away from me, refusing to meet my gaze.

I met the owner's eyes over the top of the cage. "What seems to be the problem with Elvis, Mrs...?"

"Ester," the woman said. "Polly Ester. And isn't it obvious?"

Scratching the back of my head, I looked into the cage again, only to be met with a feathered backside. Elvis ruffled his feathers and released another ear-piercing squawk.

I chuckled. "Don't worry, buddy. You're the boss here."

Careful not to disturb him, I checked for any visible signs of trauma but couldn't spot anything from outside the cage. His eyes were alert, and there were no signs of bowel issues or respiratory issues. As far as I could tell, the bird was healthy.

"I'm not seeing any immediate issues," I told Polly. "Has he been acting out of sorts?"

"Out of sorts?" she nearly screeched. "Why, of course, he's acting out of sorts! Look at him! He's so quiet."

Trying to keep my face neutral and suppress my confusion, I dropped my gaze away from Polly and focused back on the parrot. Did this woman seriously drag me over here in my off time because her bird wasn't talking as much as she wanted it to? Sure, parrots could be very vocal, but they were also temperamental and sometimes enjoyed giving their owners the silent treatment in a birdy tantrum.

I rubbed my temples as she droned on and on about how Elvis woke up this morning and was obviously on death's door because he didn't want to recap the news they'd watched over breakfast. Apparently, it was his daily routine, and for him to take one morning off meant the entire world was collapsing.

Maybe he wasn't talking because Polly wouldn't take a break long enough to give him a chance to get a word in. I was tempted to offer Polly a cracker just on the off chance it would shut her up for two seconds so I could ask more specific questions about Elvis's diet, but the woman didn't even stop to breathe.

While I didn't think Elvis appeared sick and suspected this was a case of an overly stressed owner, I wanted to rule out any other issues. I gestured for Polly to hand the cage over, and reluctantly, she stretched her arm out.

I grabbed Elvis to take him to the examination room. "If you can wait in the waiting area, I'll take him to the back to do a physical check and rule out anything serious."

Normally, I would have taken the cage and the owner into the room, but I needed a quiet moment away from her so I could think, and she didn't seem to have any plans to stop talking for the foreseeable future.

Polly harrumphed but took my cue to sit down. Her eyes narrowed as she watched me carry Elvis's cage down the hall and through a door leading to the back of the office. Somehow, even with the closed door between us, I could still feel her glare through the walls.

I blew out a long sigh, then opened the cage door. Reaching in, I let my fingers glide along Elvis's soft feathers, smiling when he ruffled under my touch.

"You don't feel very chatty today, do you, buddy?"

"Elvis chatty chat bird," he squawked. "Chatty chatty chatty chat."

I laughed. *Oh, yes. This is a clear emergency.*

At least my patient was adorable, which totally made up for the sleep I was losing.

The front door chimed, and muffled voices came from the waiting room. Elvis poked his head out of the cage door, curious about who the newcomer was. Gently nudging him back inside, I latched it and hurried to the front.

As I swung open the door leading to the waiting area, a familiar face greeted me.

"Hi, Justin," I said with a smile.

When I'd gotten off the phone with Polly, I'd called him right away. I'd assumed we had an actual emergency on our hands, but now I felt foolish for calling him in.

Widening my smile, I pointed to the back room. "Our patient is in the back."

"And who is this?" Polly asked, and I swear if she'd been a bird, she would have been ruffling her feathers like an angry hen.

"My vet tech, Justin," I explained. "Birds love him, so I asked him to come in to ensure Elvis gets the best care and most pleasant experience possible."

The answer satisfied Polly, which gave me a chance to drag Justin away before she could start a fresh stream of endless questions.

As we marched into the examination room, I noticed Justin hadn't had a chance to change out of his date clothes from the night before. My eyebrows hiked as I inspected his shirt for creases.

So I was a nosy vamp. Sue me.

Even in his rumpled shirt, Justin was a lot more put together this morning than I was, and I bit the inside of my cheek to hide my smirk when I noticed a shiny new watch on his wrist. He must really like the woman he met last night to have taken such care in every detail of his appearance. Heck, the watch alone looked like it cost a small fortune.

We walked into the room, and Justin got straight to work, making a beeline for the parrot's cage. "What did the owner say were the symptoms?"

"Polly said he's not as vocal as he usually is," I replied. "I didn't see any immediate signs of distress. Have you run across any avian disease outbreaks recently at the volunteer clinic that I should know about?"

"Nothing unusual," Justin said, shaking his head.

The clinic he volunteered at twice a month had numerous bird patients, far more than my clinic. Sunny Days tended to treat the more common household pets and the paranormal community, of course. Having Justin on staff, with his experience working with birds, was extremely helpful.

I checked on the parrot now perching on Justin's extended forearm. "He seems in good health, and he was quite talkative with me before you came in earlier."

"I'd have to agree with you." Justin rubbed his finger under Elvis's chin.

Clicking on the flashlight, I always carried in my coat pocket, I moved it from left to right. "No sign of brain trauma," I said. "But I'm still going to run blood work, just to make sure there isn't something more serious going on. Better safe than sorry. Do you mind getting the paperwork from the front for Polly, and I'll get our patient ready?"

Holding out my hand against Elvis's lower belly, I said, "Step up."

The parrot stepped onto my hand without fuss. With a curt nod, Justin slipped through the door and shut it behind him, leaving me alone with the parrot. I rubbed the bird's side with my thumb and smiled when he leaned into me.

"A star! A star!"

My brow furrowed. "What was that, buddy?"

The parrot's head turned from side to side, and while I knew it wasn't the case, I could swear I saw him try to wink. He tipped his head down, his beak disappearing into his feathers for a scratch. Shaking my head at his silly rambling, I helped him back into the cage and shut the door.

I got out what I needed to draw his blood, then glanced around for Justin. He was taking his sweet time, which was unlike him since he usually couldn't wait to leave.

Deciding I had better go check on him, I headed toward the front. When I opened the door, my heart jumped into my throat. From where I stood, I could see Justin clear as day.

His face was red, and his finger jabbed at the air between him and Polly. I froze. Polly's nostrils flared. She shouted words I couldn't make out because Justin picked that exact time to tell her to get out. However, he used far more choice words than that.

What on earth had possessed my tech? Sure, he was a bit dramatic, but he was always the definition of professionalism with our clients. My stomach churned. If I didn't step in soon, someone was going to get hurt.

Horrified, I ran toward them, putting myself directly in between. My arms spread wide.

I hissed out a quick breath before asking, "What is going on here?"

That was a mistake.

Both Justin and Polly answered at the same time, interrupting each other, which made them even angrier. That, in turn, made them louder.

Elvis must have heard them because he joined in the ruckus. "Fight to the death!" the bird screamed from the back, shouting over the two rabid humans. "Go for the jugular!"

Jaw dropping, I stared at Polly. Where had Elvis learned those words?

"My late husband used to watch wrestling with Elvis." Out of the corner of her eye, she caught a glimpse of Justin, and her face turned beet-red again. "I don't know what kind of practice you're running here, but I demand you handle this situation immediately."

Still unsure of what I was supposed to be handling, I angled my body to block my vet tech from her view and crossed my arms. My vamp hunger flared in my stomach, and I could already feel the onset of a killer headache take form at the back of my skull.

Shaking my head, I looked from Justin to Polly. "Can someone please fill me in on what happened?" When they both spoke in unison, I held up a finger. "One at a time. Justin?"

"All I did was bring over the consent form for the blood-work, and she went off on me!" Justin snapped.

"All you did?" Polly screeched. "Why would I consent to such an inhumane thing? What kind of torture chamber are you running? You're supposed to make my poor Elvis better, not worse! How would you like it if someone poked you with needles and turned you into a pincushion?"

I tried to gauge Polly's expression but realized pretty quickly that she was entirely serious. Surely, there was no way these two had nearly got into a brawl over standard clinic procedure, was there?

Either Polly was incredibly on edge and just waiting to find a victim to go off on, or something else went down when I was in the back.

I quirked an eyebrow at Justin. "You sure that's all that happened?"

"Positive," he said, his arms up defensively.

Turning to face the parrot owner, I plastered a stiff smile on my face. The gesture relaxed Polly a small bit, but she was still shaking with residual anger. Catching her eyes, I dug inside myself and did what I hadn't been forced to use in ages. I used vamp compulsion.

My irises widened, sucking Polly in—no pun intended.

"I'm sorry you had such a scare," I told the bird owner. "Do you want to sit down and tell me why you're so worried about Elvis's bloodwork?"

The woman slouched, and her body visibly folded in defeat. She teetered backward, lowering herself to sit in one of the waiting room chairs.

Justin mumbled something under his breath, but I waved him off. The last thing I needed was for him to rile her up again. Once he retreated into the rear of the clinic, I could focus on diffusing the situation.

Easing up on the compulsion, I sat next to Polly.

"I'm so sorry." She wiped the corner of her eyes. "I've been under a terrible amount of stress, and when that man—"

"Justin."

She grimaced. "Right. When Justin came over here demanding I sign off on paperwork, I just snapped. Elvis hates needles, plus I honestly can't handle any more issues right now." She glanced down the hallway to make sure we were alone. "But regardless of all that, you should think about hiring a new tech. One with better people skills."

Ouch. I always knew Justin wasn't the sweet, cuddly type, but I'd never known him to be rude. But with the way Polly was painting him, you'd think I hired a monster, which was simply not true.

Monsters weren't real.

"Elvis appears perfectly healthy, but birds are good at hiding serious illnesses. I really do believe running blood-work to check for any underlying issues is the best decision." I patted her hand and gave her a gentle smile. "So, how about this? I'll take care of Elvis's bloodwork myself and make sure he doesn't have a terrible time. Does that sound all right?"

Polly didn't look convinced.

"I'm sure Elvis is in perfect health, but we really should check everything to be sure," I urged. "For Elvis's sake."

It took a few more tries before Polly finally gave in, and I was able to leave her alone to fill out the paperwork without worrying she would destroy the clinic in her rage. By the time we finished, I knew I'd only have time for a power nap before the evening shift.

I made a mental note to talk to Justin about his bedside manner later but decided to give him the night off again. Maybe he'd had a long night with his date and needed to sleep. He'd been a good employee, so I wanted to give him the benefit of the doubt.

With a quick wave, he snuck out the back door of the clinic, avoiding Polly and preventing another confrontation. After helping her get Elvis to her car, I locked up the clinic.

By the time I'd finished, I was so exhausted I barely made it to my car. *Maybe I should put a cot at the clinic?* Because somehow, I had the feeling there would be more emergency visits in my future if I planned on expanding the practice.

CHAPTER FOUR

My feet shuffled on the pavement, and beads of sweat trickled down the curve of my back, soaking the lining of the leather jacket and making me regret wearing it. And yes, despite being a card-carrying member of the undead species, I could sweat right along with the best of them.

Most vampires had just one temperature setting—colder than a brass toilet seat in Antarctica. But for some unknown reason, I'd been born with vital signs closer to a human. In fact, it was so strange that my dad thought I'd been swapped at birth.

Every year, the man started Christmas dinner with, "I'll tell you what! If I didn't see it with my own eyes..."

He'd told the story of my birth so often it had become a staple in the Pane household. I used to be embarrassed about it—especially considering the details Dad never failed to provide—but once I became an adult, it had become another endearing thing I loved about him.

My heart gave a jolt. *I really need to make sure to call them before tonight's shift.*

Ahead of me, the turnoff for Orfus Road came into view, and I hurried my tired feet toward my car. If I really wanted to, I could have tapped into my vamp energy reserves. That would give me a boost, and I could go another forty-eight hours without sleep, but I hated relying on my powers. The best way to go undetected by humans was to keep a low profile. Besides, I worked hard not to depend on my supernatural abilities unless it was necessary.

My lips parted, and a massive yawn escaped me. If I didn't get home soon, I'd pass out right on the sidewalk.

A sharp right turn took me down the narrow alley between two buildings; it was a shortcut to the parking lot where I'd left the car. The alley smelled of garbage and rotting food, and I had to shield my nose with my hand to keep the nausea at bay. This only added to my rising body temperature, and by the time I was halfway down the alley, I was dripping wet and looking like a sewer rat.

"This is why we don't take the shortcut, Ophelia," I mumbled under my breath, then gagged as the foul odor entered my mouth.

Eager for fresh air, I picked up my pace and jogged the rest of the way.

"No!"

I skidded to a stop, feeling the asphalt scraping the soles of my shoes. Eyes wide and my chest heaving with panicked breaths, I took a cautious step in the direction the scream came from. Then stopped.

What if someone was in trouble over there?

It would be idiotic to rush into a situation without scoping it out first. I might be a vampire, but believe it or not, there could be far scarier things lurking in alleys—of both the paranormal and human variety.

The urge to wait and see if someone needed help was too strong to ignore, so I waited, straining to hear exactly where the voice was coming from.

"No!" the scream came again from the other side of the alley wall.

My breath caught. Why did I feel like I knew that voice? My answer came a moment later.

"Oh, for the love of—! Elvis, not now!"

Back pressed to the wall, I took careful steps to reach the edge of the building so I could peek around the corner undetected. The leather of my jacket brushed against the rough brick, and I could already feel the leather being scratched.

I should have jogged out of the alley like a normal person, ignoring everything that didn't involve me, but I couldn't. Keeping myself flattened and doing my best impression of a sheet of paper, I snuck a quick glance out of the alley.

Standing at the end of the street, not far from where I'd parked my car, stood Polly. She held her cell phone tightly pressed to her ear using her free hand and was balancing Elvis's cage on top of a stair railing. Other than the two of them, the small street was completely abandoned, which was the main reason I liked to park here—I never had to search for an empty space.

There were only a handful of doors that opened onto this side of the street, and most of them belonged to businesses that used the front of the building for entrance. On days when I didn't want any company, this was the fastest escape route from the chatty business owners of the main strip.

But why was Polly hanging out here when she'd left the clinic almost an hour ago? And who was she yelling at over the phone?

Guilt racked my body. I started to leave, worried I was interrupting a personal moment. But stopped when I heard Elvis yell, "No!" The bird was overly agitated, and it sent a pang of worry through me.

"Listen here, I am tired of repeating myself," Polly shrieked into the phone. "If you go through with it, you'll be sorry. I'm not telling you twice!"

What in the name of...

"Tell you twice! Tell you twice!" Elvis echoed.

Polly's frustration doubled, and I heard her exasperated sigh from my hiding place in the alley.

"I have to go before my parrot loses it," she told whoever was on the other line. "You better be careful with what you do next."

She hung up with a groan, and I listened as she fumbled inside her purse. All the while, Elvis screeched garbled words in a tone that made my ears bleed.

Huh. So much for not being vocal today.

Seconds later, Polly's footsteps reached me, and I sucked in a breath, realizing she was moving up the sidewalk and getting closer to me. What if she planned to cut through the alley back to the main street?

I needed to move, and I needed to do it fast. The last thing I wanted was to run into Polly here and have to explain why I was lurking around in alleyways like a stray cat. I'd had a hard time gaining her trust after what happened at the clinic, and I didn't need her spreading rumors about me in town or leaving us a bad review online.

My eyes scanned the area, and the realization that I was trapped hit me hard. There was no way I could make it to the main street fast enough, even if I ran. As much as I hated to admit it, there was only one thing left to do... but boy, oh boy, did I hate doing it.

Quickly slipping from my clothes, I straightened my spine and let my vamp power flood through my body. Taking a last breath, I rubbed my temples and counted to three. *Here goes nothing.*

My transformation happened in the blink of an eye, and when Polly turned into the alley a few seconds later, there was nothing of my human form left.

Unfortunately, my bat wings were weak from lack of use, and my muscles screamed in protest as I worked to keep myself afloat. This was yet another way I differed from the other vamps in town; I hated transforming.

Did I see the countless convenient ways in which someone could use their bat form to get around? Sure.

Did I understand that shifting into a bat strengthened vampiric powers? Of course.

Did I still hate it with all my being? *Abso-freaking-lutely!*

When I was young and still had vampire friends, I would join them when they practiced their shifts. We'd abandon our human forms and race into the night, playing endless games of tag while we tried to outmaneuver each other. It wasn't until I grew up that I realized how much I disliked the experience.

For starters, heights and I were not friends. Then there was the problem with the transformation hangovers I got, something that didn't seem to affect the other vamps. After staying in bat form for long periods of time, my friends would feel stronger, but I'd feel like I'd been run over by a witch's broom—more than once.

To sum it up, my normal human-like body was fine by me, thank you very much.

Which was why the first thing I did when I shifted to avoid Polly was to find the nearest fire escape railing and latch onto it for dear life. The less flying I did, the better.

Blood rushed to my head as I hung upside down, with my wings flopping around at my sides. How did Byrd make this look so effortless?

My eyes bulged as I impatiently watched Polly stomp down the alley, dragging Elvis's cage beside her until she disappeared from view. When I was certain she was gone, I let go. Spreading my wings wide, I let the wind carry me all the way to the ground.

In my head, I performed flawlessly, like an Olympic

gymnast performing a routine she'd practiced a thousand times.

In reality, I misjudged the space between the railings, banging my head and toppling toward the ground end over end until I came to a stop by face-planting on the asphalt with a hard thump.

Shutting my eyes tightly, I breathed through the shift and skulked toward the dumpster I'd abandoned my clothes behind. As I dressed, I shot a glance down the alley, worried someone would see me, but also confused about what Polly had been doing.

"This day just gets weirder and weirder," I grumbled, wiping my brow and brushing hair away from my face.

My brain was working overtime, going over every detail of the one-sided conversation I'd overheard. Who had Polly been threatening, and why?

It seemed the discussion was not the first she'd had with the person on the other end of the call, and I wondered what could have happened to cause her to react so angrily. Could that be what she'd meant when she'd told me she'd been stressed lately?

Even though it wasn't any of my business, I just couldn't shake the interaction from my mind. Pulling out my phone, I checked the time and groaned in frustration. By the time I got home, it'd be time to head straight back to the clinic again.

My body ached from the shift, and while I desperately needed to sit down, I didn't want to go back to the clinic. I needed a break from work, even if it was a short one.

Forcing my tired legs to move, I slowly made my way back to the main street and headed for the local bar. There was only one spot nearby that catered to paranormals and humans alike, and I knew I could snag a quiet booth to decompress in. My mood lifted as I headed toward the Dowsing Rod with a renewed pep in my step.

It was never too early for a Liquid Fang.

CHAPTER FIVE

I t had been some time since I'd been kicked out of a bar. The embarrassment of being escorted out of the Dowsing Rod before the sun even set was enough to make me want to crawl into a hole and never come out. Actually, I would have preferred shifting into bat form for a month straight than going through that humiliation again.

Sadly, I wasn't even drunk, let alone tipsy. Who knew that if you fell asleep with your face in an empty glass, the staff would automatically assume you needed to be cut off?

To be fair, it probably didn't help that when I tried to explain to the new bartender that I was simply tired, my mouth was stained with Liquid Fang residue dripping down my chin. Paranormal or not, Sandie wasn't having it. She scooped me up by the scruff of the neck and used her freakish troll strength to toss me out faster than I could blink.

I'd love to say the night got better after I opened the clinic, but I'd be lying. The waiting room stayed full of clients who came in a steady stream until two in the morning, and since I'd given Justin the night off, it was only me and Bree manning the place.

I stepped out of an examination room, my head spinning. "Please tell me that's the last one," I half begged the pixie.

"For now." Dipping a cotton round into a disinfectant solution, she ran it over the fresh scratches on her arm and winced.

"Mittens?"

Bree shook her head. "Muffin," she replied. "Looks like Mittens's little sister is even feistier than her."

"I'm sorry. I'll handle them next time they come in." Handing her another cotton round, I dumped the files under my arm on the front desk with a sigh. "It would have been easier if Justin were here."

My words must have jarred something in the pixie because she held up a finger and skipped toward the front office. When she returned, she held a printout in her hand and had a wide smile on her face. "You just reminded me, the results for the parrot came in."

"Already? That was fast." I took the sheet from her and read over it. "You've got to be kidding me. He's healthy, just needs a diet plan."

Bree laughed, her pink space buns shaking atop her head. "Maybe he's talking less because Polly keeps stuffing his face with crackers... Isn't it supposed to be the other way around?"

I chuckled, but I had to admit I was slightly annoyed. Had Polly seriously dragged me into the office in a complete panic over nothing?

Still, I was surprised to see his diet was unbalanced. From what I'd gathered during Polly's incessant chatter, she cared for Elvis—obsessively, even. She didn't strike me as someone who would do anything to harm him. So how did this happen?

It wasn't adding up.

I checked the results again, noting that despite being more like the older version of his namesake who loved peanut butter and banana sandwiches a little too much, Elvis the parrot was in pristine health. Despite my annoyance over my night of missing sleep, I was relieved to know nothing was physically wrong with him that diet couldn't fix. He was such a hilarious character, and one I'd love to keep seeing for many years to come.

The next thing I needed to do was to speak to Polly about the bloodwork. I debated on whether I should call her now or wait, but remembering how anxious she'd been the day before, I decided not to wait.

That way, she wouldn't think we'd forgotten about her and Elvis. After what happened with Justin, I was willing to bend over backward to smooth things out. Hoping I could leave a quick message for her to call me first thing in the morning, I dialed her number.

It took four rings for the line to connect, and I was surprised to hear Polly's voice on the other line.

"Hello?" she asked groggily. "Is this the clinic? Did you get any news on Elvis?"

Shoot. I woke her up.

Wincing, I rushed to apologize. "Sorry to call so late at night, Mrs. Ester. This is Dr. Ophelia at the vet's office. We do actually have the results for Elvis. I thought I'd get your answering machine since this isn't an emergency."

"Well, what is it then?" Polly asked, sounding frustrated. Although, maybe that was just her normal tone.

"It's—"

There was a loud bang on the other line. I paused for a moment, thinking maybe she'd dropped the phone, and then I opened my mouth to speak, but she cut me off.

"Hang on a second." Polly's breath was loud and heavy. "What in the—"

There was a note in her voice that caused a shiver of unease to skate down my spine, and I white-knuckled the phone, pressing it to my ear so hard it hurt.

"Mrs. Ester? Is everything okay?"

There was no response, and I couldn't even hear the sound of her breathing.

"Polly? Are you there?"

The line went dead.

I looked at the screen, seeing it had disconnected. When I tried to call back, the phone went straight to voicemail. My stomach twisted, knotting with worry that settled heavily inside it.

After trying to call Polly a few more times, I shoved Elvis's bloodwork results into my bag, took off my lab coat, and headed for the door. Whatever happened at Polly's had me unsettled, and my gut was telling me I needed to check on the woman. I'd do a house call under the guise of giving her a copy of Elvis's bloodwork.

Looking over my shoulder, I caught Bree's sharp gaze. "Back in a flash," I told her. "Can you handle the place for a bit?"

"I suppose," she said with a shrug. "But if Muffin comes back, you owe me dinner."

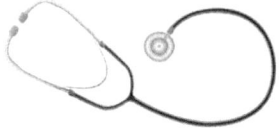

POLLY ESTER'S home was a short trip from the clinic. It sat just past the most lively parts of the town in a quiet residential area where the houses had been built in a style reminiscent of old Victorians and their flares of color.

Considering the time of night and nearly everyone being home rather than at work or running errands, it had been impossible to find a parking spot close to Polly's home. I'd had no choice but to park several blocks away and make the long trek down the street on foot to get there.

Luckily, the weather had cooled down considerably from the previous afternoon's temperatures, and the slight chill in the air was making the hike less miserable. As I walked down the wide, four-lane street, I found myself mesmerized by the shades of paint. Pink, purple, turquoise, you name it. There was even a three-story home that was painted a brilliant green that reminded me of a Red-eyed tree frog's skin. It was like walking through a rainbow.

I reached Polly's semi-detached blue house in under five minutes, and as I walked up the neatly arranged stone pathway, I scanned the surrounding area. Unlike the rest of the homes on the street, Polly's front yard was practically bursting with flowers and greenery.

Smiling, I stepped through the woven archway a few feet from the front porch. It truly felt like I was in another world. With all the trees and plants intertwining, I couldn't even see Polly's neighbor's yard, even though I knew it was directly on the other side of the white-picket fence.

I had to hand it to her; Polly had created an oasis.

Still grinning from ear to ear, I stepped up to the front porch and walked past the Adirondack chair toward the door. My hand idled in front of the buzzer, a sense of dread enveloping my bones.

Why is it so dark?

I gazed behind me at the other houses whose front porches all had lights shining brightly in the night. Tilting my head back, I studied the two sconces on either side of Polly's door; both of them had been turned off.

How strange...

Maybe she just liked to save energy? Perhaps, like me, she tried to avoid nighttime light pollution, which could disrupt migrating birds. But I would have expected her to at least have motion-activated porch lights for safety.

Reaching for the doorbell buzzer again, I stopped stock still. The door was slightly ajar.

Bluejay Falls was a safe town with very little crime, at least until the recent burglaries, but we still locked our doors at night. A shudder went through me as I poked my index finger into the wood to push it open.

A rational person would've had warning bells ringing through their heads and would have run back to their car and called the cops. But I knew I wasn't leaving until I'd checked on Polly and Elvis. Besides, after you'd taken on a troll with a cavity, there wasn't much that could truly scare you.

Squaring my shoulders, I slid through the half-open doorway and made my way inside. It was darker here than outside, and it took my eyes a moment to adjust to the low light. After a few times banging my knees against Polly's tightly arranged furniture, I gave in and activated my vamp sight. It sounded much cooler than it was, and while I still couldn't see perfectly well, I could easily see the outline of the various objects and avoid them.

Craning my neck as I walked, I inspected Polly's empty home. There was no sign of a break-in or struggle, and from what I could tell, everything was in its rightful place. The pillows on the velvet loveseat looked freshly fluffed, and I could see the curtains had been drawn for the evening. Perhaps I'd been wrong to jump to conclusions.

But if there was nothing to worry about, where was Polly?

Taking careful steps, I walked past the kitchen and toward the stairs leading to the second floor.

"Polly?" I whispered as I slowly crept to the top landing.

No answer.

Passing the bathroom, I quickly peered inside and, with my heart stuck in my throat, drew the bathtub curtain with a quick flick of my wrist. When I found it empty, I relaxed my tense stomach muscles.

Vampire or not, I'd watched one too many horror movies, and we all knew the shower was the most likely place an intruder would be hiding. *Heck!* I still showered with one eye open, thanks to those same movies.

A scratching sound pierced the silence from behind me, and I jumped. Spinning on my heels, I slunk out of the bathroom and tiptoed down the hallway toward where the sound had come from. To my left, a wall full of pictures of Elvis led the way like an airport landing strip. Step by shaky step, I crept toward the room at the furthest end of the hallway, pausing briefly in the doorway to gather courage.

After a few deep breaths and a whispered yoga mantra Bree had taught me a few weeks ago, I turned the knob and stepped inside.

This room was as dark as the rest of the house. It had a more lived-in look than the staged furniture in the other rooms, and it only took a minute to realize it was Polly's bedroom. There was a queen-sized bed against the main wall and a small antique armoire across from it. By the window stood a vintage writing desk with a curtained shape above it.

Scratch. Scratch. Scratch.

My heart lurched as the sound intensified. *It's coming from the desk.*

I moved silently across the floor toward the fabric and wrapped my fingers around the bottom hem. It felt soft against my skin, like rolled silk. With one swift swoop, I yanked the fabric down.

"Polly girl!" Elvis squawked in my face.

Barely holding back my shriek of shock, I pressed my hand to my chest and hunched over the desk being used as a cage stand to collect myself. "Sweet baby Dracula!" I told the parrot. "You almost gave me a heart attack, Elvis."

"Polly girl?" the parrot repeated, cocking his head to the side as he looked at something down by my left leg.

Yet, if this was Polly's room, where was Polly?

I followed his gaze and took a trembling step toward the edge of the bed. My knee knocked against a hard object, and I lost my balance, tumbling forward. Falling awkwardly, half on the bed and half off, I was about to tell Elvis off for leading me into a trap when I saw it.

Lying on the floor at the foot of the bed was Polly Ester. Her bare feet protruded from red pajama bottoms, and the fabric of her matching robe had a tear down its side and draped around her like a shroud or a cocoon of sorts.

My teeth began chattering involuntarily as I took in the sight of her lifeless eyes, their vacant, unblinking stare piercing through me. Swallowing hard, I struggled to suppress the gargantuan lump forming in my throat that was making each breath I took labored.

Still frozen in disbelief, I traced the contours of Polly's face, and my eyes were drawn to the stethoscope encircling her neck like a rope.

Screaming, I pushed back, tumbling onto the floor with a skull-rattling thud. It was then that I realized flashing lights lit up the night sky outside the window. Getting to my trembling legs, I pulled back one curtain to see a row of police cars lining Polly's driveway.

My heart banged around against my ribcage, and I spun around, planning to rush out the door.

A piercing white light shone into my eyes, blinding me.

"Hands up!" a deep voice growled from the bedroom doorway. "One more step, and I will shoot!"

CHAPTER SIX

T he streets blurred together outside the window of the police cruiser. My forehead rested on the glass, and I counted to ten, trying to settle my nerves. The cop who'd walked in on me hunched over Polly's dead body watched me carefully in the rearview mirror, his ridiculously long eyelashes not quite disguising the disdain in his eyes.

The grim set to the man's jaw and the tight lines of suspicion around his eyes made it clear the way the rest of the night was going to play out. There was no way I was getting out of this easily.

I couldn't blame the cop for hauling my butt into the station, considering where he'd found me. Still, a little consideration would have been great. And did he really have to lock me in the backseat like a common criminal? I would've followed him to the station in my car, but I guess that wasn't a chance they could take.

Sadly, the cops wouldn't catch the robbers terrorizing the town that night because they were too busy with veterinarians caught in misconstrued situations.

My stomach pitched as we pulled into the Bluejay Falls Police Station parking lot. A moment later, the back door unlocked, and a hand extended toward me. I recoiled from it on instinct, then, thinking better of it, let the cop help me out. One thing I'd learned from dealing with troublesome clients of both the human and paranormal varieties was that you caught more bees with honey.

"Is this going to take long?" I asked as the cop led me into the station. "I need to get back to close up the clinic."

His bronze forehead creased in frustration, and he trained his green eyes straight ahead, refusing to look at me. He was a good-looking man, I'd give him that, but I couldn't get past the self-assured attitude. Then, there was also the matter of treating me like a criminal. I bet that would be a huge turn-off for any woman.

The cop frowned. "You mentioned earlier someone was looking after it."

"Yes, my vet tech, Bree. But I can't leave her alone all night."

"We're only having a little chat." The detective's voice was cool. "The length of our time spent together will highly depend on your honesty."

My teeth clenched together, and I battled the urge to

argue. Was this man implying I would lie? What reason would I have to do that? I'd already explained my presence in Polly's house and how I'd found her. The more time I spent with the detective, the more I suspected he had it out for me. It was almost like he wanted me to be guilty.

There goes my trust in our town's security.

The front door swung open, and the smell of bleach burned my nose and made my eyes water. Bluejay Falls Police Station was a cramped building with a small reception area that held only one desk behind a wall of clear plastic. A row of tattered leather chairs sat to the left of the desk, and a long corridor that led to closed rooms was to our right. The eerie atmosphere gave me the creeps, and it didn't help that this was the direction the detective led me.

As we passed the reception area, a young cop watched me through narrowed eyes, clicking a pen on the battered desktop.

"Room three open?" the detective leading me asked.

The young cop nodded, his gaze never leaving me.

Honestly, now. It's not like I'm some serial killer.

Rolling my eyes, I brought my sleeve to my nose to keep the sharp smell that seemed to permeate the station from suffocating me. The last thing I needed was to end the night by emptying my stomach all over a cop. I couldn't imagine he'd appreciate my dietary preferences, and I really didn't want to explain them.

The detective noticed my grimace. "It doesn't usually smell this bad. There was an incident earlier."

I shrugged. I didn't need to know what could have occurred that would have required this much cleanup. More than that, I definitely didn't need to make small talk with the arrogant buffoon dragging me in for questioning.

Shoulders tense, I followed the detective into the small interrogation room. My head throbbed as I lowered to sit on a metal chair with metal cuffs dangling off the handles. The thing was about as cozy as a bed of nails and had clearly been designed to make criminals as uncomfortable as possible.

I leaned my elbows on the cold tabletop, trying to ignore the violent churning in my stomach. How long has it been since I drank? My gaze flicked unbidden to the cop's neck artery. Catching myself, I averted it instantly. *Too long*, I wagered.

"Am I under arrest?" I asked, my voice tight.

"Not at all." Tall, dark, and annoying winced. "My name is Detective Ryder Wolff. I'm sorry for not introducing myself earlier."

I tilted my chin. "Ophelia Pane."

"Yes, you mentioned that back at the crime scene." I cringed at the words *crime scene*, but thankfully, Detective Ryder continued, saving me from dwelling on it. "I understand you must be frustrated, but I'm sure you can understand that, considering the situation, there is a protocol we must follow. We have a team at the scene, and once we can corroborate your story, you'll be free to go."

Gulping, I stretched my legs out, accidentally bumping

Ryder's under the table. He pretended not to notice. Typical power play. Refusing to let him win, I pushed my feet as far as they would go without my butt sliding off the chair. It was childish, but I was too hangry to stop myself.

I lifted an eyebrow. "So, kind of under arrest, then?"

"Believe me, Miss Pane, if you were under arrest, you'd know it," Ryder stated flatly. "Now, can you please tell me why you were at the victim's home so late at night?"

A groan escaped before I could stifle it.

Ryder's eye twitched, and he placed his cell phone on the table between us, clicking a key. "For the record, this time."

Speaking as clearly as I could and trying my best not to get upset, I once again recounted my steps for the evening. I told Ryder about the clinic and how it only operates in the later hours, the alarming phone call with Polly, and what I found at her house when I arrived. I even quoted everything Elvis said, which I didn't think was needed, but hey, the more information I gave the detective, the better the chance he'd see I had nothing to hide—except for the whole vampire thing—and would let me out of here faster.

Ryder Wolff was like a dog with a bone, and as I spoke, I could feel his metaphorical teeth sinking into my words, looking for even the faintest whiff of a lie.

Nice try, buddy.

I was as clean as a whistle.

My stomach growled, and the intensity of my hunger pains had me folding nearly in half.

Across from me, Ryder's bushy eyebrows rose an inch. "We can take a short break if you need it. There's a vending machine in the lobby if you want to get a snack."

Unsure how to tell the man the snack I needed couldn't be found in a regular vending machine, I only shook my head and forced a meek smile to my lips.

"Look," I said, leaning on the edge of the table. "I know how this looks, but it truly is a wrong place, wrong time situation. I didn't even know Polly outside of meeting her at the clinic. What reason would I have to want her dead?"

An image of Polly's lifeless face flashed before me, and my chest tightened. The events of the night were catching up with me, and now that I had some time to think, I wasn't sure how much longer I could keep myself together. As a vet, I was used to handling difficult situations, but this was so much worse than anything I'd ever encountered.

Bella Lugosi! I saw a dead person today.

I tried to recall the last time I was in the same room as a corpse, and nothing came to mind. While the concept that vampires were immortal was a complete myth, we did live significantly longer than the human population, so I'd never even attended a funeral.

My parents were both in perfect health, and Grandma and Grandpa were nowhere close to kicking the bucket. Mom constantly joked that those two would outlive us all. I had to agree with her. For a couple well into their nineties, they sure lived it up. Right now, they were on a cruise somewhere near Thailand and had already reserved a two-month trip to Australia when they returned.

Which was probably why seeing Polly rattled me to my very core. Goosebumps spread across my skin, and I rubbed my palms against my arms, trying to ward off a sudden chill.

"Did you hear or see anything when you were with the victim that implied she may have been in danger?" Ryder asked.

My pulse sped up as I recalled the phone call in the alley. How would I tell him about it without making myself look like a stalker? More so, how would I explain my batty escape? Swallowing the knot in my throat, I settled on the vaguest version of the truth I could come up with. "I overheard her having an argument with someone on her phone after her first visit. But I made out very little of it."

"I'll need you to write down what time you thought the call happened before you leave," Ryder said. "Anything else you think I should know?"

The argument she had with Justin in the clinic about Elvis's bloodwork popped into my mind, but I wasn't sure if incriminating my vet tech would be helpful. Besides, I highly doubted Justin had killed Polly over such a petty thing. He'd been too caught up in his date.

An image of the stethoscope around Polly's neck caused my mouth to go dry and my vision to blur. *It couldn't be...*

"Miss Pane?"

I rubbed the back of my neck. "Polly and my vet tech had a disagreement over the treatment of her parrot. But it's probably not relevant."

"I'll be the judge of that," Ryder said sternly. "Is this the same vet tech in the clinic now?"

I shook my head, and he slid a notepad my way with a pen attached to it. "I need their name and phone number, please."

Had I just implicated Justin in a murder? I tried not to think about it. With a shaky hand, I wrote down his number from memory and slid the notepad back to Ryder. His eyes scanned the name. He ripped off the paper, folding it neatly into his uniform pocket.

Clearing his throat, his gaze locked on me. "Can you think of any other occurrences that struck you as odd?"

This entire thing is odd.

"Not really," I said slowly. "As I mentioned before, I only spoke to Polly briefly, and it was about her parrot. Speaking of Elvis, what will happen to him now? Birds require specific care."

"Usually, in cases that involve pets, they go to the nearest available shelter."

My eyes bulged. "You cannot put Elvis in a shelter. Most shelters aren't equipped or prepared to deal with exotic pets."

"I'm afraid we can't keep him here, Miss Pane." Ryder appeared genuinely apologetic.

Before I could stop myself, I offered, "I can take him. At least until someone else can come forward to claim him. I'm assuming you will notify next of kin about what happened to Polly?"

"Of course," Ryder said.

Relief washed over me, and I nodded slowly, never breaking eye contact with him. "Good. You can tell them Elvis needs a good home to go to. Hopefully, someone in Polly's family or a close friend will be able to care for him the way she did."

"She really loved that bird, huh?"

I smiled. "That was the impression I got."

Across from me, Ryder readjusted his weight in the chair and tapped the tip of the pen on the table. His jaw tensed as he reached for the phone, clicking the recording off before pocketing it.

"Well, in that case, thank you for offering to house him for the time being," the detective said. "I think we're all done here."

"I'm free to go?" The hopeful note in my voice was embarrassing, but I was too hungry and tired to care.

Ryder's chest rose and fell, and I tried not to think about how wide it was. "For now. Though I wouldn't leave town if I were you." His lips quirked. "In case I have more questions."

With that, he stood up, leading me out of the room and into the lobby. He grabbed a set of keys that looked an awful lot like mine from the reception desk and handed them to me. "I had an officer bring your car here after the crime scene team finished with it. You'll find it parked just outside."

Leaving the station, I found the sun had just begun to rise and checked my watch. If I hurried, I could still make it to the clinic in time to help Bree lock up. I could already picture the questions the pixie would have, and while I didn't wish to relive the night again, filling her in was the least I could do for ditching her tonight.

At least I'd be getting home at a proper hour this morning. Which was wonderful, because I didn't think I had ever wished for a full day's sleep more.

CHAPTER SEVEN

My rest was not as beneficial as I'd hoped. I spent the day tossing and turning as every sliver of light that shone through the bedroom blinds made my eyes snap wide open. Even in my sleep, I couldn't get the image of Polly out of my head. Deep in my heart, I knew it would be a long while before I could forget it. If ever.

By the time I rolled out of bed, showered, and picked up Elvis from the police station, I was running behind. Luckily, I found a parking space close to the clinic rather than parking in the usual lot.

I jogged toward the clinic with the birdcage rattling in my hands. Elvis screamed bloody murder with every jarring bump, which made Byrd, who was hiding away in my purse again, hiss in aggravation. Everyone who spotted me at that moment probably thought I looked like a complete lunatic.

Hushing them both, I scrambled in my purse for my keys and slid inside the door, locking it behind me. After flicking on the lights, I checked the schedule for tonight, and my shoulders sagged in relief when I saw there were only two appointments on the calendar.

Bree and Justin both asked for this night off weeks ago, so I was on my own for the shift. I wished I hadn't agreed to it, but I always tried to be a good boss. Besides, how could anyone have known I'd be saddled with an angry parrot today?

As if on cue, Elvis shrieked, "Elvis big mad!"

Rolling my eyes, I opened my purse wide to let Byrd fly out. The bat flashed his fangs at me briefly before scurrying off into the deep crevices of the clinic, not to be seen again until he wanted his nightly snacks.

I stepped closer to the cage, inspecting Elvis to make certain he was all right. "I know you're in a mood because you miss your owner, but can you try to keep it down? Please?"

"Down! Down!" Elvis shrieked. "Down she goes!"

"I'll take that as a no."

Turning my back to the cage, I walked to the reception desk and flipped through the patient charts for the two appointments. One was a simple checkup for an older cat that would be a breeze, but the other required a bit more work. The paranormal kind.

On any other day, I wouldn't have minded helping a

troll pull a rotten tooth. Tonight, though, I really wished I had backup. Even with a good sedative, trolls tended to get easily aggravated, and considering their size after a shift, I hated to think I'd be handling one alone. Especially this one. Skeeter Kraus was a big man in his human form, and he was even bigger as a troll.

I need to remember to double up on the sedatives this time, I thought.

Closing the folder, I made my way to the rear of the clinic, where we kept the medication locked up. Years ago, when I first opened the clinic, I'd hired a friend to design a secret compartment in the cabinet for paranormal supplies, one that could only be opened by a special key card. Since Bree was paranormal, I had one made for her as well, but Justin didn't know about this part of our storage room.

Moving quickly, I unlocked the cabinet and pushed aside some boxes to reach the rear, then fished into my coat pocket for the key card.

"What the...?"

The pocket was empty.

I checked every inch of my lab coat and even the scrubs I often wore and came up with nothing. Where had I left that card? My brain worked overtime trying to recall the last time I'd seen it, and I gasped, realizing it was on the night I'd gone over to Polly's.

Having rushed over there in a hurry, I hadn't bothered changing out of my work clothes.

"No, no, no," I whispered into the empty room.

Could I have dropped the card somewhere in Polly's

home? Surely, if Officer Wolff had found it on the scene, he would have returned it to me by now? Or mentioned that he had it. I hadn't heard from him since the interview, and no one had said a word about it when I picked up the parrot today, which led me to only one logical conclusion.

The card was still at Polly Ester's home.

It was imperative that I retrieved that card before my shift started. I never knew what emergencies I might be dealing with on any given night. However, if a hysterical hellhound showed up needing surgery or a gryphon with a broken wing landed on my doorstep and I couldn't treat them, the town was going to have worse problems than burglaries on their hands.

But I couldn't exactly ask Detective Ryder for it either, not unless I wanted to risk him asking questions. Questions I couldn't answer unless I wanted to break paranormal secrecy laws or just have him think I needed a grippy sock vacation for believing in mythical creatures.

Checking that Byrd wasn't causing chaos as a protest to having his quiet life interrupted by Elvis, I headed for the door. There was still just enough time before the clinic opened to give me the opportunity to get to Polly's and back. What I was going to do when I got there was another story, one I would worry about later.

But there was no way I was taking on a troll with a bad tooth without supernatural-strength sedatives.

As expected, Polly's home was sectioned off with enough yellow police tape to be seen from the moon. I parked my car in the same spot as last time and made the trek over, nearly biting my nails to the bone with each step. When I neared the house, I stopped in my tracks.

"Shoot," I hissed under my breath as I stared at the police cruiser in the driveway.

When I picked up Elvis, I got the impression that the cops had finished with her place, but it appeared I was wrong. The chances of me getting into the house and searching for my key card without raising suspicion were slim to none. No doubt if I asked the officer marching up and down the front porch to let me inside, he'd call Ryder, and I had absolutely no desire to see that man again.

Temping down my rising frustration, I focused on the task at hand. I could wait until the cop left and sneak in, but I didn't know when that would be. Besides, if I was caught, Ryder wouldn't waste a single second in arresting me for breaking and entering. I was sure of it.

That left only one option.

I pulled back my hair into a high ponytail and strutted up to the house with false confidence. My hips swayed from side to side as I climbed the steps, but the instant the cop stationed on Polly's porch turned around, I regretted my decision. It was the young man who'd been manning the desk when Ryder had brought me in for questioning.

If I was hoping not to be recognized, that chance was shot to bits before I could even blink.

The cop's eyes narrowed on me, and he placed one hand on top of his gun holster.

Great. What exactly did Ryder tell these people about me? He said I was free to go, so why is this cop staring at me as if I'm murder suspect number one?

Annoyance blossomed in my chest, and my body flushed with the desire to march straight into the station and give Detective Ryder a piece of my mind. But before I could do something I'd regret later, I put on my friendliest face and waved.

"Can I help you?" Officer Grumpy Face asked.

While I hated to use my vamp abilities for selfish reasons, this instance called for them. I could deal with the fallout of my conscience later, but right now, I needed inside that house.

The flow of blood slowed in my system and my eyes widened, the irises darkening as I stepped closer to the young cop. His shoulders drooped, and he drifted toward me on instinct; the compulsion took its hold. The kid didn't stand a chance.

I smiled sweetly, resting a hand on his shoulder. "So sorry to trouble you," I cooed. "But I don't believe you're meant to be here. Best to get going before the boss finds out. And forget you ever saw me here. Okay?"

"R-Right. Y-Yes," the cop stuttered.

Without another word, he brushed past me and stormed off the porch. I watched him get into the cruiser and drive away, waiting until he was out of sight to head for the door.

Slowly, I turned the handle and exhaled. "Unlocked."

Squeezing myself through the narrow opening as though I was made of liquid, I tiptoed into the house, checking every corner for police officers. I doubted anyone else was here, but one could never be too careful when breaking and entering.

Although, was it really considered a B&E if the door was open? I shook my head. It didn't matter, because if Ryder caught me in here, he'd assume I was committing a crime, and the semantics wouldn't make any difference.

If Mom and Dad could see me now, they would never let me live this down. Miss Goody Two Shoes suddenly acting irresponsibly? Who was I turning into?

Reminding myself that this was for the greater good of not getting tossed around like a toy by a troll later, I followed the steps I'd taken through the house the night I'd found Polly. There was no sign of the keycard in the living room or in the hallway leading to the bedroom. With only one place left to check, my hope of finding the key was quickly fading.

Rushing into the bedroom, I worked to push the memories of Polly's body to the back of my mind as I checked the floor for signs of the lost card. My cheek pressed to the hardwood bedframe as I peered beneath it.

Nothing.

About to give up, I turned away from the bed when Elvis's cage caught my attention. When I'd picked him up this morning, he'd been in a portable cage similar to the ones that shelters used, so I'd assumed the cops had an animal control team here to gather his things and take him from the house. Knowing Elvis, he'd probably caused a heck of a ruckus.

My eyes flashed to a sliver of white inside the cage.

Careful not to disturb anything, I reached inside and lifted a corner of the cage floor liner.

"Aha!" I yelped excitedly, spotting the card.

It must have fallen out when I lifted the cover off the cage and slid under the liner when they evacuated Elvis. Either that or the bird had hidden it on purpose, something I wouldn't put past him.

As I plucked the card out, my fingers grazed a hard edge tucked toward the rear of the cage bottom. Sliding my hand further under the liner, I gripped the flat object with two fingers and pulled it out slowly, my lips parting as I lifted it out of the cage.

In my hands was a small, leather-bound notebook, the type old-school reporters carried around in their jacket pockets.

I chewed my lip as I studied the book. "What on earth is this doing here?"

A loud beeping sound pierced my ears. I jumped at the sound of my phone alarm going off. I had programmed it earlier in case I got carried away in my search, so I knew when it was time to call it quits and get back to the clinic.

Luckily, I still had a bit of time left, but I had to hurry if I was going to make it back in time for my first appointment. The notebook felt heavy in my hands, and after one quick glance at my phone, I sucked in a breath and flipped through the pages.

No one ever said curiosity killed a bat.

My vision narrowed as I turned the lined pages. I couldn't make sense of anything written here. From what I could gather, I was looking at dates and times, but what for? I had no idea. And since there were at least four pages filled with them and I was in a hurry, there was no point sticking around to think about it now.

Cramming the book into my purse, I cursed myself for not being better at puzzles, then headed for the door.

Once I stepped onto the front porch, I felt instantly at ease. The cop I'd sent away hadn't returned yet, and I was pretty certain he'd be gone for a while.

Compulsion tended to muddle people's memories. It would be a hot minute before he realized he'd left. More often than not, everything in the few minutes before a human was compelled by a vampire was completely forgotten. No one knew why that happened, but I always assumed it was part of the process to make sure the vampire's identity stayed a secret.

Whatever the reason, it would certainly work well in my favor today.

Checking the street for witnesses and finding none, I bolted toward my car. As I climbed in, my heart jolted with excitement. I may have been terrible at solving puzzles, but I knew someone who could help. And it so happened that I was on my way to see them.

CHAPTER EIGHT

Skeeter Kraus was a towering figure with a gargantuan frame that dominated the room, and his personality was as big as his physical appearance. His wide-set eyes followed me around the room as I readied the sedatives—four, to be exact—their gaze holding an intensity that seemed to slice through the air like knives.

The examination table groaned ominously under his considerable weight, straining to stay upright. I hadn't dared to weigh Skeeter since it had cost a fortune to fix it after the unfortunate incident the one time we'd attempted it, but it was clear he had only grown larger since our previous encounter. The man was at least seven feet tall, and both his height and weight were pushing every conceivable boundary.

The funny thing about trolls like Skeeter was that they defied the conventional rules of aging—they didn't stop growing as time passed. However, in Skeeter's case, his growth seemed particularly pronounced, a fact that was impossible to ignore as he glowered down at me.

I put the final needle on the table, my mind circling. The notebook I'd found at Polly's continued to gnaw at the back of my brain. I hated that I couldn't figure it out on my own and felt guilty that I was even considering dragging Skeeter into this. Then again, the man owed me from when I'd saved his bacon after he accidentally catapulted himself through a shop window down the street from the clinic.

It had taken significant convincing and a round of strong compulsion, but Mr. Seltzer had finally agreed not to press charges. He'd also conveniently forgotten about witnessing Skeeter's face changing into his troll form.

So, yeah, the giant owed me one.

Skeeter raked his thick fingers through even thicker, jet-black hair. "On a scale of one to I-want-to-die, how much will this hurt?"

"The shots?" I asked, trying hard to suppress my chuckle. He couldn't be serious.

His eyes flashed with worry. "I'm not great with needles."

Positioning my body so I blocked his view of the needles, I placed a hand on Skeeter's large arm and patted it. His shoulders drooped, and he tested his jaw, the motion making the swelling from his bad tooth appear to be even larger.

"I promise this will only be a few pinches, and when

you wake up, you'll feel a million times better," I assured the troll. "Don't you want to be rid of the pain?"

"It's the other pain I'm worried about," Skeeter replied.

I'd wanted to wait until after the procedure to ask for Skeeter's help with the notebook, but judging by how jumpy he was, I wasn't sure he'd be up for it later. Plus, I didn't know how he'd react to the sedatives. The last troll I'd treated had been up and full of energy within the hour, but you never knew in these cases. Skeeter could be asleep till morning, or worse, never go down at all, and I'd have to fight an angry troll for the rest of my shift. If that happened, I definitely wouldn't be able to ask for his help.

The thing with trolls was not only were they impressively massive, but they were unbelievably talented at deciphering codes, which was why most bedtime stories featuring trolls had them living under bridges and asking people to solve riddles for the fun of it. Sure, I didn't know a single troll who spent their time doing that anymore, but it was still part of their history. They were all very good at solving everything from simple riddles to the most intricate of puzzles.

Take Skeeter, for example. He might be afraid of a little jab, but there was no human living on this side of the equator who was better at numbers than he was. There was a reason the troll was a cryptologist and why he was in high demand for his groundbreaking encryption and decryption research. Last I'd heard, Skeeter was working in cybersecurity, but that was all he would say about it. If anyone could help me find out what the dates and times in the notebook meant, it was him.

I stretched my spine so I could be closer to eye level with Skeeter. "Hey, before we start, do you think you could take a look at something for me?"

"Absolutely!" The bench groaned again as Skeeter scooted closer to the edge, clearly eager to seize any opportunity to delay getting jabbed.

He glanced at the clock on the wall, and then his eyes slid past it to the tall bookcase Byrd was hiding in. At least he had curled into a little ball and wasn't flapping around the waiting area and scaring the humans tonight. Skeeter's lips twitched into a side smile as he registered the bat's presence, and he chuckled under his breath.

"I see the little guy is still here," Skeeter said.

I'd almost forgotten that Skeeter was here when Byrd had first shown up. That had been a shift I had thought would never end, with patients coming in and out like a rotating door. I had just opened the clinic, so I'd been working alone, without a vet tech to help lessen the load. Not to mention, I'd primarily had paranormal patients that night, which came with unique challenges.

When a tiny bat had flown through the rear door and terrorized the patients waiting, I'd nearly burst into tears, thinking I was going to go out of business before I'd even had a chance. Luckily, Skeeter had been there to help me get the clinic under control. While I'd dealt with seeing as many patients as possible, he'd lured Byrd into a storage closet and had calmed him with treats and rolls of towels to curl up in.

Come to think of it, Skeeter was one of the first paranormals I'd met in Bluejay Falls who I considered a friend.

I looked between the bat and the troll. "He's a permanent fixture now."

"No surprise there. I knew from day one there was no getting rid of him." Skeeter's large eyes narrowed on me. "So what's this you want me to check out? You in some kind of trouble, Lia?"

"Not at all," I said, slightly too defensively. "I found a notebook with some numbers in it, and it has me completely stumped. I figured you might enjoy solving a puzzle."

The troll's eyes glittered with excitement. "Well, quit teasing me and hand it over then."

"You don't have to analyze it now," I told Skeeter, reaching for the book in my purse on the chair behind us. "But in case you're sleeping it off for a while, I thought I could leave it with you."

As Skeeter skimmed through the rows of numbers, my pulse sped up. I wasn't sure why, but I was desperate to find out what it all meant. Moreso, I wanted to know why Polly had hidden the stupid thing in the cage, but I guessed that the mystery would have to wait to be solved. If I was smart, I'd hand the notebook over to Officer Wolff. So why hadn't I?

Because then you'd have to explain how you got it.

I scratched my chin, frowning. Judging by how things had been going with Ryder thus far, he'd have me locked up for tampering with a crime scene. My best bet was to find out if the notebook was even relevant to Polly's death before I got myself entangled in more trouble. Chances were the numbers meant nothing at all, and I could forget all about it.

"This is strange," Skeeter murmured, delicately flipping the pages between his large fingers.

Every muscle in my body grew rigid. *Oh, boy.*

I closed some of the distance between us so I could look at what he was pointing at. "Strange how?"

"These numbers... I thought they were familiar, but I can't place my finger on it," the troll said. "It's a stretch, but it's the only connection I can see."

Following the movement of his finger, I pushed my face closer to the page, reading out the dates he pointed to. They made as little sense to me as before. Whatever Skeeter saw, I wasn't seeing it, which wasn't all that surprising, considering numbers were his thing, not mine.

Peering up at him, I arched one eyebrow questioningly. "You might have to dumb this down for me."

"You see these?" Skeeter said, turning the notebook around and circling one set of dates with his nail. "It's the day the toy store in Stoneville was robbed. And this one"—he pointed to another line of numbers—"that's the Money Mart robbery in Gloutchester."

"Are you saying all these dates are from the recent robberies?"

It couldn't be. There were hundreds of entries here,

some stretching as far back as several years ago. Was Skeeter implying every single date related back to a robbery that had happened? That would put the count in the double digits, and I didn't recall hearing anything about that on the news.

"I don't know about all of these," Skeeter answered, "but I can definitely pick out a good dozen. Where did you say you got the book from?"

I gulped. How would I explain to him I'd found it hidden in a dead woman's house? I didn't want to drag Skeeter further into this mess, especially now that I knew some of the dates corresponded with crimes in nearby towns. My heart raced in my chest. Why on earth would Polly have this notebook?

A thought tickled the back of my brain, and I eyed Skeeter. My throat was suddenly tight, and my mouth was dry. "Do you recognize any dates that match the robberies in Bluejay?"

"Definitely," the troll said with a curt nod. He pointed out a few in the notebook, and my blood ran cold. "This one is from last month when that zoo got hit. Then there's the used car dealership that was broken into during the summer. Oh, and this one here is for the convenience store on Flytrap Lane."

My lungs froze, making it hard to breathe. "Did you say Flytrap Lane?"

When the troll nodded, I leaned on the side of the examination table for balance. That was Polly's street. In my hurry to get in and out of the house, both times I'd been there, I'd failed to notice any stores nearby. If what Skeeter said was true, that would mean a robbery happened right down the street from Polly.

My eyes widened into saucers.

And she had the date written down in a secret book.

A million theories swarmed my mind. I swatted them away, trying not to jump to conclusions. Was Polly Ester somehow responsible for the robberies? And if she was, was that the reason she wound up dead?

I had always assumed the robberies were the work of more than one person; they were too organized, too well planned. Now, looking at this book and seeing how many dates were scribbled in it, my blood turned to ice. I grabbed the notebook from Skeeter and tried to smile, hoping he wouldn't see my panic.

Polly had hidden the book for a reason. An insurance policy, perhaps? Maybe she was using it to protect herself in case the other criminals she was working with decided to turn against her.

No matter what the reason, one thing was certain. Polly wasn't the sweet parrot owner I thought she was, and I was the only person who knew it.

CHAPTER NINE

I woke up on the couch with Byrd curled up at my side, his tiny body warming my skin. Orange cheese puff dust sprinkled his dark fur, and when I looked at the couch cushions, I saw little orange prints from where he'd climbed up onto the sofa. On the coffee table, a ripped-open bag spilled out, and pieces of junk food spread out on the surface.

The rascal had gotten into the stash of snacks I'd hidden away from him again.

With a smile, I slid around the bat like a ninja and got to my feet. Rubbing my eyes, I checked the time. It was only three in the afternoon, but there was no way I could go back to sleep.

Across from me, the sunlight streamed into the living room through a slit in the curtains, illuminating the mess on the floor. I must have been dead tired after last night's shift because I hadn't even bothered putting my things away. My purse lay open on the rose-colored carpet, with all its contents spilling out of it.

Casting one more glance at the snoring bat, I bent over to pick up my bag. As I lifted it, the notebook I'd found at Polly's tumbled out, and the corner of the spine landed on my toe. Wincing, I bit down on my lower lip to keep from yelping, not wanting to wake Byrd up. I didn't need him flapping around for the next few hours.

My fingers curled around the leather, and I sat down cross-legged, aimlessly flipping through the pages.

"Why did you have this, Polly?" I whispered to an empty living room.

As if in answer, my eyes caught on the date of the convenience store robbery on Polly's street. I frowned. If Polly was the one running these awful schemes, why would she risk taking on a place next to her home?

It seemed not only risky but especially foolish. From what I'd gathered so far, considering how long it had taken anyone to even catch the robbers, they weren't the foolish type. Another thing that was glaringly obvious after a good night's sleep was this had to be a team. No way could one person organize a thieving ring that had been going on for years.

I ran my finger down the page of numbers. "Who were you working with? Did they turn on you?"

Bottling up my theories, I stared at the same date again. My heart had begun to beat wildly in my chest, and the anxiousness I was trying to suppress reared its ugly head.

At this point, I knew myself too well to think I would leave this alone. I could pass the information to the cops, but what if they just botched it up? Or worse, decided to pin the entire thing on me?

I gritted my teeth and jumped to my feet. It was time to stop sitting around and do something.

Taking long strides, I crossed the living room and jogged to the kitchen, where I downed two boxes of Crimson Quench like they were going out of style. Then I put on my shoes and slipped out of the door.

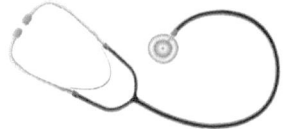

The Grab 'n Go convenience store loomed in the distance as I strode down Polly's street. To my right, I watched her house grow larger, and my stomach tensed at the sight of the yellow tape crisscrossing the front yard. I sped up and reached the store before I lost control and emptied the contents of my belly on the sidewalk. One sure way to announce to the human world that paranormals existed was to make some poor person clean up two liters of a vampire's blood lunch off the asphalt.

Gross.

I shook my head at the nauseating thought and turned to face the convenience store. My eyes burned from the garish shade of yellow the walls had been painted. Tilting my head back, I squinted against the afternoon sun to study the giant sign atop the brick building. From where I stood, the Grab 'n Go was an eyesore on an otherwise quaint and cozy street.

"How did I not notice this place before?" I grumbled, moving toward the entrance.

My hand jiggled the handle that nearly broke off in my grip, and I pulled on the iron-bar-clad door to get inside. The first thing I noticed when walking in was the camera above my head. A flashing red light blinked at the top, and I immediately regretted not thinking of using a disguise. What if the police looked at the footage and saw me here?

I didn't dwell long on that possibility, as I was quickly distracted by the state of the store. If I were a claustrophobic person, this place would be a living nightmare.

The entire store was made up of rows of shelves that stretched so high up they almost touched the ceiling. Each shelf was packed to the brim with random items that didn't appear to be organized in any sort of discernible pattern. To my left, a coffee machine that looked to be older than my oldest ancestor whirred to life, wheezed out a few drops of brown liquid, then sputtered and died again. I tightened my jaw, searching around me until I spotted the cash register in the far corner of the store.

It looked abandoned.

I made my way toward it, dodging stacks of paper towel boxes on the floor. Maneuvering through the store was akin to walking down a maze in a horror movie. I half expected a masked man wielding a chainsaw to jump out from behind a shelf. For the life of me, I couldn't picture Polly even stepping foot inside the shop, let alone robbing the place.

When I reached the register, I pressed my nose to the acrylic barrier that protected it and frowned. Was anyone working?

A head popped up behind the barrier, and I clutched my chest, barely managing to swallow a scream.

"How can I help you?" the short man asked.

As his gaze rolled over me, I realized he was looking for a change in my features, though I couldn't be sure what for. The man's beady eyes landed on my jeans, and a realization hit me. He was trying to see if I was armed. The robbery must have done a number on him.

Now that I had paid more attention, I could see that the barrier protecting him from me was new, and the camera above the door was clumsily bolted in place, as though it had been attached there in a hurry.

I forced out the warmest smile I could muster. "Hi there. My name is Lia. I was a... friend of someone who lived on this street."

"Oh! Well, why didn't you say so?" The man ran a bony hand over his receding hairline. "The name's Tim Burr. Proud owner of this fine establishment. I always love to hear my place comes highly recommended."

My smile faltered, and I hurried to hide any signs of what I actually thought of the store's unique decorating style. The last thing I wanted was to hurt Tim's feelings. He seemed to be a sweet old man, and it was horrible to think someone had broken in here and stolen from him. People were selfish monsters.

"Yes, Polly said you made quite the impression on the street." It was disturbing how smoothly the lie rolled off my tongue.

Tim's gaunt face paled. "Not Polly Ester? The poor woman." He reached under the counter to pull out a cloth handkerchief, dabbing it under his eyes. "You know, I've been a permanent fixture on this street for decades, and I have to tell you, it sure has taken a turn for the worst lately."

This is my in!

"I agree. Polly mentioned you were one of the unfortunate ones who got hit by the robberies."

"Sure was!" Tim reached over and tapped his knuckles on the barrier between us. "Had this put in right after, can never be too careful these days. It was the first time anything so awful happened. Needless to say, the entire street was up in arms. And now with Polly…"

He brought the handkerchief to his eyes again, his mouth down-turned. While Tim collected himself, I tried to think of the right words to say to make him less anxious. No one ever told you this when you decided to devote your life to treating animals—and in my case, paranormals—that after spending so much time with them, you forgot how to handle people.

I could comfort a hurt animal or calm a hormonal were-wolf, but humans were a different kind of challenge. Especially if you were trying to squeeze information out of them on the sly.

Luckily, I didn't have to think about it long because Tim was more of a chatterbox than he'd originally let on. He cleared his throat and pocketed the handkerchief, leaning in over the counter until his forehead nearly bumped the plastic.

"I don't usually like to get involved in community business," he said. I bit back the snort that bubbled to the surface because Tim was a gossiper if I'd ever met one. "But some folks on the street say Polly might have brought this one on herself."

"Oh?" My eyebrows shot up into my hairline.

"I know how it sounds," Tim added quickly when he saw my shocked face. "You have to understand. This is a quiet street. Most folks here don't want to be disturbed, and Polly was a great fit. At first. Then she brought that bird home, and it all went downhill."

Come again?

I scratched my neck, piecing the implications together. "Are you saying someone might have wanted to get rid of Polly because of her parrot?"

The front doorbell rang, and I stretched my neck to see who had come in. A woman in her midthirties with a toddler in tow came barreling in, heading straight for the back aisle, where a large refrigerator unit took up the bulk of the wall. She ripped open the door, grabbed a massive carton of chocolate milk, and rushed to the register.

I stepped aside to give her a wide berth and waited patiently while Tim rang her up. The two spent a couple of minutes on small talk until the little boy got antsy and pulled at the woman's messy bun. Excusing herself, she left the store in the same fashion as she'd come in—like a tornado.

Perhaps the street isn't quite as calm as Tim would have me believe.

"That was Nancy," he said, though I didn't ask. "Her husband is gone all month for work, and she's been having a time with the kids."

I nodded. "Must be hard to manage. Was she one of the people who didn't like Elvis?"

"Elvis?"

Right. I tended to forget most people didn't memorize the names of every pet in a ten-mile radius like yours truly.

"Polly's parrot," I told the store owner. "You mentioned the neighbors had an issue with him."

"Neighbor," Tim corrected. "Sure, some talked, but no one hated that bird more than Dusty. She lives in the house next door to Polly's, and from what I recall, the two didn't get along. Dusty didn't like the bird being too loud and interrupting her meditation business."

"Her what now?"

The store owner smirked at me through the barrier. "Dusty is one of those new-age meditation instructors. Made a fortune a few years ago when she started an online business teaching people how to get connected to their inner selves. A bunch of bologna if you ask me, but it sure seems to pay well."

Doing my best not to rush the man, I waited while he gathered his thoughts and spoke again.

"Anyhow, Polly and her used to get into it fiercely enough that the entire street knew about it. One time, I could hear them arguing all the way out here. That's how loud they got! If you ask me, they were much more disruptive to the peace than the parrot ever was. No matter what Dusty said, I like the little guy."

"And you think Dusty could be mad enough to take drastic measures?"

The color left Tim's face, and he took one step back, putting distance between us. His lip quivered, and for the first time, it appeared that the man was fully aware of how much he had said.

"I wouldn't go that far," he corrected. "Chances are what happened to Polly was a tragic case of the wrong place, wrong time. Same as when the store got robbed."

I was about to tell him that the robbery was likely calculated, but we were interrupted by the front door bursting open again. This time, it was an older gentleman who made a beeline straight for Tim. The two said hello in the fashion of longtime friends, and I had the feeling that my chat with the store owner was coming to an abrupt end. Before I could get roped into their lively conversation about the storm threatening to hit Bluejay Falls next week, I thanked Tim and scurried outside.

The sun shone from above, not a cloud in the sky. I paused to reapply my sunscreen, a triple layer of SPF 100 and looked down the street. From here, I could barely make out Polly's house around the bend in the road.

Whatever argument she and Dusty had had must have been a bad one for Tim to hear it all the way out here. My eyes flicked to the small red-brick house beside Polly's, then to my watch.

Half an hour until I needed to head back. Plenty of time to pay Dusty a visit.

CHAPTER TEN

Dry leaves crunched under my feet as I trudged up the overgrown path leading to Dusty's front door. On either side of me, the barren bushes lined the path, their dry leaves crunching beneath my shoes. This was the only front yard on the street that looked as though it hadn't been cared for in years.

The grass was patchy and brown, the flower beds were empty other than clumps of thorny weeds, and there was a tacky iron sculpture of a dog doing its business under a sad-looking tree. The words "Stay off!" had been hand-painted across the dog's back, the paint smearing at the edges.

This was exactly the type of yard you expected a monster to have, and everyone knew you only approached monsters with pitchforks and fire… not when you were alone.

Grimacing, I was about to turn around and hightail it out of there, but thoughts of Polly kept me going. That and the fact the police were clearly barking up the wrong tree, meant I had no choice but to press forward with my own investigation. The faster I figured out what really happened to Polly, the faster I could get them off my back.

My balance faltered as I climbed up the crooked steps of the front porch, and my eyes strayed to the large bay window. Through it, I could see inside the house clearly, and it was in no better shape than the yard. The furniture was mismatched, and appeared to be older than Father Time himself. There were strange tapestries taped up on nearly every wall, and I was willing to wager they were being used to hide holes in the walls that needed patching.

Didn't Tim say Dusty was a meditation guru? Nothing about her home gave me a calming sense of relaxation, and, as far as I knew, that was the main point of the practice.

I steadied my wobbly feet and pressed my finger to the doorbell. When I pulled my finger away, it clung slightly, thanks to something sticky on the buzzer's surface, and I fought to keep from gagging.

"Coming!" a sharp voice echoed from inside.

A few seconds later, the door flew open, and I was met with a curious set of pale green eyes. A woman in her late sixties stared me down, her braided hairstyle coming undone as she cocked her head to the side to inspect me.

Dusty's heavily lined eyes traveled down my body, and I saw the wheels turning in her head while she tried to make out who I might be. On her neck, half a dozen crystal necklaces clanged together, the noise too chaotic to be peaceful.

"Dusty Strangler," she said, extending a freshly manicured hand. "Are you here about my meditation consulting? Because that is strictly online."

I shook my head. "Oh no. I'm here about your neighbor. Polly Ester?" Realizing I hadn't introduced myself, I reached for her hand and shook it briefly. "My name is Lia."

A dark cloud passed over Dusty's features, and she stepped away as though I'd burned her with my statement. Her eyes narrowed, the pupils shrinking visibly. For a second, she reminded me of a feral cat.

"I really don't have time for this," she said coldly.

Dusty moved quickly, and as the door began to close, I saw my opportunity vanishing before my eyes. Unable to stop myself, I threw my foot out, cramming it in the narrow space between the door and frame. A low thud sounded as the wood slammed into my shoe, and Dusty jumped back from the shock of having possibly maimed me. I didn't believe either of us expected me to be so forward.

Sheepishly removing my throbbing foot, I smiled like an idiot. "I promise it won't take much time at all."

"All right, fine," Dusty huffed. "But I'm not sure what you want from me. If this is about what happened, I already spoke to the police. Wait, are you a cop?"

"Veterinarian, actually," I admitted. "Elvis was a patient of mine."

The mention of the parrot had Dusty's mood toggling from bad to worse. Her shoulders hiked up to her ears, and she sucked in a sharp breath. I found myself half expecting smoke to pour from her nostrils like an angry dragon. Her back uncurled, a rigid straight line forming in her spine. Even the air around us felt tangible and thick, as though Dusty's feelings tainted it somehow. She closed the door an inch, watching out for my still aching toes.

"That bird!" was all Dusty said.

"I take it you weren't a fan?"

"Ha!" the woman barked out. "Listen, I'm not saying I'm glad about what happened. Heaven knows everyone on the street knew how I felt about Polly and that demon bird. But I sure am glad to have some peace back again. Another day of the beast's incessant squawking, and I was going to lose my damn mind. He wasn't so bad when she first got him, but it progressively got worse. Unbearable, if you ask me."

Note to self: meditation does not work for everyone.

I wondered if Dusty's clients knew how she behaved in real life because I was pretty certain she wouldn't be able to hold on to them for long if they found out. Somehow, I got the distinct impression Elvis wasn't the problem here.

My blood boiled thinking of how much hate the woman had for a poor, innocent creature. I hadn't known him long, but Elvis was a gentle, vivacious parrot. A bit chatty, sure, but not exactly the evil nuisance Dusty was describing. Then again, I didn't live next door to him.

"A lot of times birds react negatively to change, and it can spark a shift in their behavior." I worked past my feelings toward the parrot hater and met Dusty's gaze. "Have you noticed anything out of the ordinary next door that may have aggravated Elvis? Maybe new people showing up or Polly acting especially anxious?"

The woman tugged at one of the crystal necklaces, rubbing it between her index finger and thumb.

"Not that I noticed," she said. "But I don't spend my days watching that lunatic and her bird. There must have been something off, though, all things considered."

I paused. "Which things do you mean?"

"You know, the whole"—she made a noose motion with her right hand—"or whatever it was."

"You don't believe it was a coincidence? Wrong place, wrong time?"

Dusty waved me off. "Of course not! Aside from the robbery a while back, we don't get much crime in this area of town, or in Bluejay Falls, for that matter. If what the cops said is true and Polly was killed, she brought it on herself. The woman was insufferable. Just like her bird."

I bit down on my tongue before I told Dusty that the only insufferable person I saw here was her. The nerve of the woman to trash Polly so soon after her death. Some people were simply too self-concerned to care about others —another reason I was sure Dusty's entire business foundation was a sham. People like her were exactly why I preferred spending my days with animals.

I tried my best to gloss over her gross behavior and stay on track. "So you haven't seen anyone visiting Polly or hanging around the neighborhood in the last few weeks that stuck out?"

"Nope." Dusty shrugged. "But I can ask Tristan if you like."

"Tristan?"

"My son." The woman twirled the crystal again and growled deep in her chest when it got caught in a tangle on another chain. "He's been doing some work fixing up the yard for me, so he'd have had a better view of Polly's place. He's coming by later today. I can check with him then."

Letting go of the crystal, she pointed to a row of picture frames on the wall beside her. I poked my head through the opening of the door to see a tall, handsome man in his twenties. His wavy blonde hair was a shade of gold so bright he appeared to glow. Behind the glass, the man's gray eyes followed me as I scanned the other pictures. One of him with his arm around Dusty in front of a giant mural. One where he was casually reclining on a shiny black motorcycle, his leg kicked up like a movie star on set. The last portrayed Tristan holding up a wineglass to cheer the camera, his full lips parted in a half-smile.

"Handsome kid," I told Dusty.

She beamed with pride. "One thing his deadbeat father did well was supply the good-looking genes. My boy sure is a heartbreaker."

"You must be very proud. And I'd really appreciate it if you could ask him about anything he might have noticed next door." I rubbed the back of my neck, straining to look beyond the yard toward Polly's place.

Whatever work Tristan was doing in the yard, it didn't

show. I could barely make out the sidewalk in front of the house with all the bushes in the way. No way would he be able to see anything from here, and while it was nice of Dusty to offer to check, I highly doubted anything would come out of it.

Even if Polly did have new visitors in the weeks prior to her death, I didn't think a stranger killed her. The way I'd found her…

Whoever wanted Polly dead had a grudge against her. The crime was too personal to be anything else.

One thing I had to agree with Dusty on—this was not a random crime.

"When was the last time you spoke with Polly?"

"Me? I have no idea," Dusty replied. "Probably last week. It's no secret we had it out again over the parrot. Polly wanted to bury the hatchet. I told her I would as long as she kept that obnoxious bird quiet."

"Did she agree to the truce?" Her continued insults about Elvis had me biting the inside of my cheek hard enough to draw blood in an effort to keep my anger under control.

"She did. But nothing changed." Dusty folded her arms over her chest, her frown deepening. "Look, this stays between us girls, all right? The police know, but I don't want the street talking about me. The day before Polly died, I had about enough. I filed a petition with the town council to have the bird removed."

My eyebrows nearly hiked up to my hairline. *So much for a truce.*

"You wanted them to euthanize Elvis?" I asked, unable to keep the horror from my voice.

"You make it sound like I'm a monster. You have no idea what it was like living next door to that thing. All day and all night, non-stop. It was driving me crazy!"

I backed up a step, trying to get away from her as she pushed her face closer to mine. From this angle, with Dusty's eyes bulging with anger and her mouth seething, she was the definition of unhinged. Whatever Elvis had done to make her so angry, she wasn't joking around. Dusty was truly off the rails.

"As I said," she hissed, her voice low, "it's a shame about Polly, but I'll tell you one thing: I've never been happier! Good riddance, if you ask me."

The thought of spending another second in the company of this heartless woman made my skin break out in goose-bumps. A shiver tripped along my spine, and I fought the strong urge to tell her off.

Elvis was lucky not to be around such a vile human being another minute longer. Thinking of him back at the clinic caused my heart to ache over what the poor guy had gone through. I'd have to make sure to show him some extra love tonight to make sure he knew there were plenty of people out there who adored his chatty personality.

Not bothering with pleasantries, I told Dusty not to worry about asking her son anything and bid her goodbye. Dusty's eyes left searing marks on my back as I retreated, and I held my breath until I heard her door close behind me. I forced myself not to run as I hurried away from the negativity of the so-called meditation guru.

The sound of something falling over made me stop dead in my tracks.

I tilted my head, my neck twisting toward Polly's. Was it me, or had that sound come from her backyard?

Still frozen mid-step, I checked the driveway for a police car, but it was empty. The house was deserted. Then what had I heard?

My body reeled with the decision of what to do next. I could pretend nothing happened and head back to the car. That was definitely the smarter choice. Or...

Unable to stop myself, I crouched low as I left Dusty's front yard and took a sharp left up the sidewalk toward Polly's house. Smart or not, I was going to see what was out there, even if it killed me.

I was so lost in thought I didn't even notice the person coming toward me. Not until my forehead banged against a hard chest, knocking me backward onto the sidewalk. I rubbed the sore spot on my forehead and tried to clear my blurry vision, so I could make out the dark shape standing over me.

What fresh steaming pile of dog crap have I stepped into now?

CHAPTER ELEVEN

A s my vision slowly returned, the world
sharpened into focus, and I found myself unable
to do anything but gape in disbelief. Standing
before me was none other than Tristan himself, the prodigal
son in the flesh.

In person, Tristan appeared more imposing than I had
imagined after seeing the photos. With his large frame
towering over me, I couldn't stop myself from shrinking
away from the shadow he was casting on me. He wore a
snug green sweater that seemed to strain against the fabric
as he moved, accentuating the chiseled muscles of his chest
beneath it.

Tristan's piercing gray eyes swept over me with a cool
intensity that sent a chill licking across my skin. It was
beyond strange for my body to react like this, especially to a

human. I was a fang-toting vampire and far from defense-less, so why was I so intimidated by this guy?

For a fleeting moment, a wild thought crossed my mind: perhaps Tristan possessed supernatural abilities that I was picking up on a subconscious level—a shifter, maybe. I instinctively sniffed the air, seeking any trace of the magic that typically clung to our kind. But all I could smell was the aroma of dead leaves and wet soil from Dusty's front yard.

I rubbed the growing bump on my forehead, staring up at Tristan. "Sorry about that," I mumbled with what I hoped was a smile. "I didn't see you there."

"Not a problem." His face remained as emotionless as a stone. "Are you a friend of Mom's?"

I glanced at the house over my shoulder to make sure Dusty wasn't there. "Sort of. I came by to check how she was doing after what happened to Polly next door. Make sure she's all right."

It wasn't entirely a lie. Not really. At least, that was what I told myself, and I tried to hide my burning cheeks that were probably turning a brilliant crimson.

"You're Tristan, right?" I continued. "Dusty's son. Your mom is very proud of you."

The young man chuckled, and the sternness in his features evaporated. Perhaps Tristan was a gentle giant, after all.

Lips twitching, he widened his smile and offered a hand to help me up. "That's me! And you are?"

"Lia," I said, letting him pull me to my feet and then

shaking his hand. His fingers were massive, closing around mine. "Lia Pane. I was Elvis's vet."

Tristan arched a bushy brow. "The parrot?"

No, I'm Polly's vet. Duh.

I fixed my face before he put the walls back up. "Yes. He could be a bit loud, huh?"

Tristan shifted his weight, and a brief darkness flashed behind his eyes. In a second, it was gone, and those gray orbs sparkled again in the sunlight. *How odd.*

I guess the apple hadn't fallen far from the tree when it came to Tristan and his mother's hatred for their next-door neighbor's bird.

"He was all right," the young man said, surprising me. "Mom can get obsessive over things, but she means well. Anyway, I wasn't here enough to be annoyed by him. I doubt he was as bad as she says."

"He's not," I agreed, surprised and slightly confused. Had I misread the darkness that had glinted in his eyes? If he didn't despise Elvis, then what had caused it?

I cleared my throat. "Hey, did you happen to see anything strange when you were here? Dusty mentioned you've spent some time out here fixing up the place recently. Notice anyone snooping around who shouldn't have been?"

Bristling, Tristan looked at the house, then back to me. "Other than Mom, you mean?" he said with a harsh laugh. "I'm only joking. But no, nothing weird around here. This street is as boring as they come, to be honest."

He rolled up a sleeve and looked at his watch, a gold

chunky one that looked expensive. "Now, if you don't mind, I really need to get going. My girlfriend will kill me if I'm late for the movie again, and I still have to check in with Mom."

With that, he flashed me a dazzling smile, revealing a perfect row of white, glistening teeth that seemed to sparkle like a toothpaste commercial in the sunlight. He cast a swift wave goodbye as he hurried toward the house, his footsteps echoing against the pavement.

With Tristan's departure, my anxiety dissipated, allowing me to focus on the task I'd set out to accomplish before bumping into him. I still needed to uncover the source of the commotion next door. With a renewed resolve, I darted down the pathway toward the neighboring home.

Each step I took was infused with a mixture of curiosity and determination, propelling me forward with a sense of purpose.

It took longer to snake around Polly's house than I'd expected, mostly because I had to stop to reapply sunscreen mid-way. I hadn't anticipated the added time this trip would take when I'd left the house earlier, and the bottle of SPF in my purse was running low. Leave it to me to end up with a raging sunburn while I was out snooping. I looked at the lobster-color skin of my exposed forearm and pulled the sleeve of my light jacket lower.

No doubt I would pay for this later.

On cue, my stomach growled, and the sound echoed down the narrow path skirting around Polly's home. I jerked my gaze around to make sure no one was nearby to hear it, relief flooding through me when I realized how hidden away from the world this part of the garden was. No one would find me here unless Polly's murderer was here in the garden with me already. What if he or she had come back to the crime scene, and that was the noise I'd heard?

On second thought, perhaps this wasn't my most brilliant idea.

Another loud noise drifted from the backyard, and I stopped breathing. My back flattened against the brick wall behind me as I crept slowly toward the direction the noise had come from. No matter what the fairy tales told you about vampires, we weren't all made for danger and lurking around in the shadows.

Sure, some vamps loved being creepy, but not me. I preferred a cozy, quiet existence where I wasn't stumbling over dead bodies in the middle of the night. And yet here I was, running headfirst into yet another stupid situation.

Maybe Mom was right; I really did need a lesson in self-preservation.

Another loud bang had my legs quivering. The hairs on my arms rose, and I steadied my breathing, imagining the meditation sessions Dusty led.

In and out. In and out. You got this.

My brain refused to be fooled by meaningless words while I was slinking ever closer to danger. I certainly did not have this.

By the time I reached the end of the wall I pressed against, I was a sweaty wreck. My hair stuck to my forehead, the springy curls falling into my eyes and making it impossible to see clearly. My shirt clung to my wet back like Saran Wrap under my jacket, and my knees locked with every shaky step.

All in all, I looked an awful lot like Byrd that time he'd knocked a toilet lid closed and trapped himself inside it.

A part of me wanted to stay positive and convince myself I could simply rely on my vamp abilities if there was, in fact, a killer in the backyard. But I knew better. Since I tried not to use my supernatural skills if I could help it, I wasn't all that great at using them. Especially not at the drop of a hat.

Should the killer come at me, I'd get staked before I even realized I was in danger. Honestly, with vampires like me around, it was a surprise we hadn't gone extinct centuries ago.

A dragging sound filled the backyard a few feet away from me.

Closing my eyes tightly, I breathed in through clenched teeth and rolled my shoulders. It was now or never. Gathering all my courage, I took the first step forward, my eyes still shut. As I rounded the corner, I peeled one lid open, then the other.

My breath got caught in my throat, and I gave a strangled cry of shock.

Sitting atop an overturned garbage bin was the largest, angriest orange tabby I had ever seen. Its fur was matted in a sticky substance, and when I looked at the bin, I noticed the same gooey mess dripping down its sides. Two green eyes tracked my every movement as I walked slowly forward.

"Here, kitty, kitty, kitty," I sang softly as I neared the possibly feral animal. "I'm not going to hurt you."

Daring to move closer to the cat, I kept my steps light so as not to scare it. Being a vet with a ridiculously tender heart, I always had a couple of treat bags in my purse for these types of emergency meetings. Although, from the looks of this cat, it was no stranger to eating. Seriously, this fluff ball was larger than a werewolf pup.

My gaze stayed locked on the cat as I slowly reached into my purse to pull out one bag. As soon as the treats were out, the cat was in motion.

Everything happened so fast that I barely had time to register it. One second, I was standing in the middle of Polly's backyard, dangling a bag of cat treats, and the next, I was on my back with an enormous orange ball of fur sitting on my face. I sputtered, sucking bits of the sticky fur into my mouth as I did.

Rolling over, I gently pushed the cat off my face so I could breathe. It hissed as it landed on the grass at my side. Its mouth was full of cat treats, and its claws were extended, ready to protect the tuna-flavored loot. I scurried backward on my butt before I got my eyes scratched out for trying to be helpful.

With me out of the way, the cat hissed again, grabbed the bag with its sharp teeth, and rushed out of the yard. As if on purpose, the cat kicked the garbage bin with its hind legs on its way out, and the stupid thing rolled in my direction, slamming into my thigh.

Grunting, I got up and brushed away the remnants of dirt and garbage from my jeans. "Can't save every princess."

The stench of old garbage overpowered my senses, forcing me to pull my shirt over my nose to stop from gagging. On the plus side, other than the cat, the backyard was clear. The noise I'd heard earlier was probably the tabby knocking the bin around. Casting one final glance over the yard, I turned to leave.

As I passed a tall hedge on the outskirts of the yard, my nose picked up another scent. My stomach clenched.

I knew that smell.

Going against my better judgment, I pulled my shirt down and gave the yard a deep sniff. My vamp sense of smell was stronger than most animals', and as soon as the air filled my nose, I knew exactly what it was. Cloves and pine.

"Justin's cologne," I whispered to the empty yard.

What the heck was Justin, my vet tech, doing in a dead woman's backyard? Terror ripped through my body as I recalled the argument the two had in the clinic.

No way.

I refused to believe it. There was absolutely no chance Justin would kill Polly over a disagreement about bloodwork. It was so bizarre I refused to even entertain the idea. But then, why had he been here? In her home, or at least in her garden?

Scanning the yard, I tried to take in every detail. Maybe it was a coincidence, and someone else wore the same cologne as Justin.

Turning in a circle, I surveyed everything around me. The backyard was fairly normal, aside from all the garbage currently strewn about. There was a small deck right off the main house with a round table and two chairs. A BBQ grill stood near them and dangerously close to the back door of the house. In the far-right corner was a small shed, and when I checked the door, I found it was locked. The space was fairly small, and the leafy shrubs that ran around its perimeter made it appear even smaller.

My eyes trailed over the grass, which was surprisingly well cared for. Unlike Dusty's place, there wasn't a single patch missing, and except for one section near the hedge that appeared to be flattened out, the green covering Polly's backyard was lush with life.

I walked toward the trampled part, then stopped in its center. "Hmm."

Standing here, I had the perfect view of Polly's kitchen and living area.

My heart raced in my chest. "Was someone watching you?"

Just then, the alarm on my phone went off, and I scrambled to get it from my purse to turn it off. It was time to head back. I was already cutting it close, and I still needed to get home to pick up Byrd.

Starting for the exit, I lifted my boot and groaned. It seemed the cat had done more damage than I'd thought to the place because I'd definitely stepped in a wad of chewed-up gum. Pulling a tissue paper from my bag, I scrubbed at the nasty residue, but it wouldn't budge.

I should have been annoyed, but another emotion over-took me. My nose twitched as the smell of wasabi perme-ated my senses. Mouth gaping, I looked from the gum on my shoe to Polly's house. While there was a chance someone else wore the same cologne as Justin, the idea that they also chewed his brand of obscure gum was too coin-cidental.

There was no denying it. My vet tech had been in Polly's backyard, and he'd been here recently.

"Why were you spying on her, Justin?" I asked the empty garden, not really sure I wanted to know the answer to my question.

CHAPTER TWELVE

"A little help, please!" Bree's words were little more than a squeak through the exam room door.

I finished administering ear infection drops into a tiny Chihuahua's ears before gently depositing him into his owner's arms.

"Excuse me for a moment, please." Wiping my brow, I opened the exam room door and stared.

On the other side of the waiting room, Bree stood with her arms tight against her sides. A snake shifter coiled around her until very little of her body was visible.

"Help me!" she wheezed as the snake squeezed tighter, and she struggled to stand still.

"Are things like this normal?" the woman whose dog I treated asked, peering around me.

I laughed sheepishly. "More often than you'd imagine."

"Well, if that's all, I think we'll be going. See you in two weeks for Percy's follow-up!" The woman clutched her trembling dog and rushed out of the clinic.

Shaking my head, I made my way toward Bree. Her face was starting to turn red, and I knew if I didn't coax the shifter off her soon, we'd have big problems. Most shifters kept at least a portion of their humanity when in animal form, but the snake—who had to be Bob since he was the only serpent shifter in town—seemed to be completely checked out.

I placed my hand on his sleek, scale-covered body. "Bob, I'm going to need you to let my tech go."

Nothing.

Either Bob couldn't hear me, or he had it out for the pixie. Since this was his first visit, and Bree hadn't told me about any recent run-ins with a cranky snake shifter, I doubted it was the latter. Sliding my hands along Bob's muscled coils, I found his head and gently began unwrapping him from Bree's body. The snake shifter flicked his forked tongue in my direction and hissed.

"Now, Bob, listen here." I booped his nose, and he jerked his head back with an annoyed huff. Deciding to try reason, I summoned my most coaxing tone. "I can't help you if you make my tech pass out. We need her. Can you please be a dear and untangle yourself so I can get a better look at your cut?"

Reluctantly, the snake obliged. Little by little, he uncurled his long body from around Bree. The moment she was free, Bree gulped in several giant breaths, still holding the snake in her arms. Winking at me, she carried Bob into the closest exam room and deposited him on the metal table.

I followed her into the room and began running my fingers across Bob's stretched-out length, studying his injury. "How did this happen, Bob?"

Bob turned, rising off the table until we were at eye level. I remained still as he pressed his forehead to mine. There was a faint static electric shock, and then images flashed through my mind as Bob used his magic to show me what had happened.

From what I gathered, he'd been puttering around his yard when the neighborhood kids set off fireworks, and the sudden noise scared him into shifting. Unfortunately, he'd been holding garden shears and had landed on the sharp blade when he shifted.

I took my time cleaning and dressing the wound. "This will take some time to heal," I told the shifter. "It isn't deep enough to need stitches, though; consider yourself lucky. I'm going to send you home with an antibiotic to prevent you from getting a nasty infection. Take your time collecting yourself in here, and when you're ready, you can shift back. Is there someone who can come pick you up and bring a set of clothes?"

The snake hissed and pressed his forehead to mine again, a name and phone number flickering in my mind.

"Good. I'll have Bree call your wife. Once you're in human form, feel free to use one of the robes over there." I pointed to a shelf of freshly laundered robes I'd had Bree order after the werewolf situation. "We'll send your wife in when she arrives. No more gardening for a while, all right?"

Another hiss.

"You're welcome," I said. "Next time, try not to strangle my techs, though. Okay?"

Bob nodded his head, and with a laugh, I left the room, Bree following on my heels.

When I closed the door, Bree spoke. "Bob was our last patient. I can lock up the clinic if you want to get out of here early."

"Are you sure?" I asked.

Bree nodded. "Of course. You haven't had a day off in weeks." She smiled. "By the way, have you talked to Justin?"

Her words caught me off guard because I had been thinking about Justin quite a bit since this afternoon at Polly's house. He wasn't due for another shift until tomorrow night, but it wasn't like him not to check in at all. Sure, he wasn't as committed to the clinic as Bree was, but he usually called in to make sure we weren't swamped when he'd been off several days in a row.

It was probably a coincidence. At least, that was what I told myself. I didn't even want to think about the other option, which was that Justin had killed Polly for whatever reason and was now on the run.

I shook my head, refusing to believe it. "I haven't talked to him since the emergency visit with Elvis."

"Speaking of... Elvis keeps repeating his owner's name."

Hating the idea of Elvis being alone while grieving Polly's death, I offered, "I'll take him home with me. I could use the company anyway."

Making my way to the back of the office, I gathered my things. A yawn escaped before I could stop it, reminding me of how much my body needed a chance to relax and catch up on sleep. But despite being exhausted, I knew I wouldn't be able to sleep today—not with thoughts of Justin swirling like a tornado in my mind.

I hated that I couldn't trust my own vet tech. If I was going to get any peace at all, I had to talk to Justin and get some answers. I was sure this was nothing more than a misunderstanding, and the sooner I could clear it up, the sooner I could get some rest.

Grabbing Elvis's cage on my way to the door, I yelled a quick bye to Bree and headed outside, with my next stop weighing heavily on my heart.

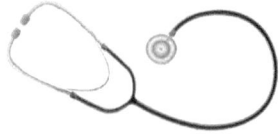

Justin Case's apartment building sat on the edge of town, right off the highway. It had all the makings of a luxury condominium, but the sparse landscape covered in construction equipment and dirt, combined with the lack of amenities nearby, made it appear more depressing than fancy.

"A star has a center!" Elvis squawked from his cage, strapped in on the backseat.

I turned around and glanced at him. "Be right back, okay?"

"A center has a star!"

"I'll take that as a yes," I told the parrot, who watched me with beady eyes.

Leaving my car running, I climbed out and walked at a clipped pace to the main lobby. The sound of cars zooming by on the freeway behind the building was almost bursting my eardrums.

When I first moved to Bluejay Falls, this area had been referred to as an up-and-coming neighborhood where all the out-of-towners flocked to, wildly interested in the prospect of owning a vacation spot close to town. It wasn't until years later, when no other developer settled on the land, that the reality of the place became clear. If you enjoyed a life of complete solitude, Razerhall Apartments were the place for you. Otherwise, you were better off renting one of the B&Bs in the more central locations. There was even a spot that got booked out years in advance because of its proximity to the falls.

As I stepped through the grand revolving doors, crossing the threshold of the building, the aura of big money enveloped me. The transition from the bleakness outside to the opulent inside was nothing short of remark-able. The massive lobby opened before me like a palace, each element meticulously designed to exude luxury and sophistication.

Imposing leather sofas were strategically arranged around an enormous marble fireplace, commanding the attention of anyone who entered. Their rich hues contrasted elegantly with the polished marble, and I found myself running a finger along the side of one sofa, if only to check if it was real. Spoiler alert, it felt like butter.

The sheer scale of the lobby, which was approximately the size of a football field, was breathtaking. Towering windows stretched from floor to ceiling, framing a row of tiny trees lining the outside. Against them stood three potted palm trees, their leaves lightly swaying in the slight breeze of the silent air conditioning.

Adjacent to the bronze elevator doors to my right was a cascading water feature that added a soothing natural sound to the otherwise cold and empty space. Despite its secluded location, this building seemed destined to one day be a hub of social activity and a gathering place for the elite.

A knot formed in my throat. Though I made it a point to compensate my techs well, I was by no means paying them enough to afford an apartment here. I was pretty certain my entire house couldn't pay for a down payment on one of these units.

Swallowing hard, I checked my phone for Justin's contact card and made a beeline for the elevators. The building was quiet, and it took me by surprise when the doors opened and a mother with a baby stroller came barreling out.

She gave me a once over and offered a fake smile before rushing out, running over my foot in the process. I squeezed myself against the wall, trying to get out of her way, and stumbled into the elevator. Pressing the button for Justin's floor, I hurriedly jammed the door close button just in case the stroller attacker returned to finish the job. Soft jazz played on the speakers the entire way up to the fourteenth floor.

The elevator came to a smooth stop, and the doors slid open without even a whisper of sound. Stepping out, I looked right and left, trying to orient myself and figure out how the apartment numbers were organized. After a few failed attempts, I was finally on the right path and could see the number for Justin's place a few doors down. I rapped my knuckles twice on the deep mahogany door and waited while my insides knit themselves into knots.

Silence was the only thing that greeted me.

I raised my hand and tried again, this time knocking louder. "Justin? It's Lia, are you home?"

When that failed to summon him, I slumped forward and rested my forehead against the door. The dim hallway lent to my dreary mood, and I couldn't stifle the lump of anxiety forming in my chest, no matter how hard I tried to assure myself I was overreacting.

Where is he?

"You looking for Justin?" a gruff voice asked.

I peeled myself away from the door and spun around. Behind me, peering out from the suite opposite Justin's, stood a tall young man in a long silk robe. His hair was wet as though he'd just stepped from the shower, and he held a tall glass of green juice. The man raised his arm to lean on the doorframe, and the robe parted slightly.

My cheeks burned with the fire of the sun.

The man, however, was not in the least bit bothered.

"Um, y-yes," I stuttered. "Has he been home today?"

Quirking an eyebrow, the man shrugged, causing the robe to shift. I locked my wide eyes on his face so I didn't have to see any more of him than was absolutely necessary.

"That depends," the man drawled. "Are you a girl-friend? Because I don't want to get him in trouble."

"I'm his boss."

"Oh. His *single* boss?"

Someone kill me now. Seriously, stick a stake in me because I'm done.

Battling the urge to roll my eyes, I crossed my arms and summoned my coolest professional mask. Not bothering to answer his inappropriate question, I asked, "Have you seen your neighbor? It's important I speak with him."

"All business," the man said with a smirk. "I like it. But no. I haven't seen Justin in days."

Interesting.

I tried to keep my head from spinning with wild theo-ries. "Do you usually see him a lot?"

"Definitely. Matter of fact, he totally bailed on me last night. We were supposed to grab some beers, but Justin was a no-show."

"Is that normal for him?"

The man shook his head. "I figured he was out on a date

and got carried away. Justin is always out with someone. Now me, on the other hand—"

"All right, thanks for the info!" I cut him off, not wanting to know where he was about to take this conversation. "If you do see Justin, let him know Lia is looking for him." I spun around to leave, then, unable to help myself, turned back. "And put some pants on, for heaven's sake."

Putting more distance between me and the slimeball neighbor, I speed-walked to the elevator and shifted my weight from foot to foot while waiting for it to arrive. When the doors finally parted, I poured myself into the tin can and clung onto the brass railing for dear life.

In the mirrored wall, my reflection stared back at me, reminding me that my poker face sucked. My expression showed every worry and suspicion that was on my mind. Justin Case was missing, and the last time I saw him, he'd been arguing with a woman who was now dead.

Could I have been wrong about Justin? Was there a possibility that he'd gone back to finish his fight with Polly, and things got out of hand?

As much as I didn't want to believe it, it was too much of a coincidence to believe Justin and Polly weren't somehow linked. Justin had to be more deeply involved than I'd realized.

My fingers white-knuckled the elevator railing. Was my vet tech a prime suspect in a murder? And was I the only one who was seriously looking at him?

CHAPTER
THIRTEEN

My head was a muddled mess that I couldn't seem to clear out. And now that I was away from the hustle of work, I couldn't think of anything other than my suspicions. Flopping down on my couch, I tried watching television, but got lost in my thoughts after two minutes. I picked up a book, but that didn't work either. Normally, a good storyline was enough to distract me, but not today. Today, no matter what I tried, all I could think about was Justin and Polly.

By some miracle, I managed to sneak in a few hours of restless sleep. When I woke, I dragged my tired behind into the shower and stood under steaming hot water until it turned cold and my skin had taken on a prune-like texture. Still, my head throbbed, replaying the scenes from the last couple of days over and over.

With the clinic opening in a few hours, I couldn't afford

to allow my distraction to cloud my judgment. I had to be in tip-top shape if I was going to take on patients because there was no way I would risk the well-being of a sweet little creature by not being fully present.

There was only one other place I could think of to go to decompress, which was how I found myself driving the all-too-familiar winding road past the farmhouses that flanked the outskirts of our quaint town. Coming close to my destination, I turned down a smaller road and slowed down.

In the distance, the Bluejay Falls Library, nestled like a beacon atop the hill, calling to me. The old Victorian-style building, with its weather-beaten facade, stood as a proud piece of history.

Along the road leading to the parking lot, large weeping willows lined the path with their graceful branches swaying gently in the breeze. Their low-hanging leaves fell like delicate lace, creating a canopy that filtered the sunlight into dappled patterns on the ground below.

As I neared, the soft rustle of leaves and the distant murmur of a nearby stream drifted into the air. I rolled down the windows all the way so I could hear it more clearly and allowed it to wash over my frayed nerves.

I'd been coming to the library since I first discovered it upon moving to Bluejay Falls. Eager to learn more about my new home, I'd been out driving early one morning and had made a random turn that led to the library. Sadly, when I rushed into the library that morning, I hadn't been searching for higher knowledge but rather for a bathroom after having downed too many blood boxes on my drive.

Luckily for me, I would find a place to empty my bladder and so much more.

Since the second I stepped foot in the library, I knew I would come back to it time and time again. Being surrounded by tall, spanning shelves that all held worlds of possibilities, along with the smell of antique paper and aged leather, called to my soul. I'd been an avid reader from the moment I'd learned to string words together to read a full sentence, but this place... It had real wonder hidden inside it.

My mind was still racing when I parked the car and made my way to the library entrance. I could feel my heart lighten as I wrapped my fingers around the brass handle and pulled. Soon, I would be comfortable in a leather armchair and lost in a fantastical story that was far from my daily life. I had the distinct feeling that was exactly what I needed to get my head on straight before work.

"Work your magic, you brilliant beast," I whispered to the library, pulling the door open.

The interior of the library was a quirky blend of traditional and modern designs. The architecture, with its high ceilings and ornate moldings, spoke to a past era, while sleek, contemporary furniture and state-of-the-art technology had been integrated into the space to make the library more relevant to younger visitors.

The main reading room was, as always, a sweet spot to relax in and almost entirely empty. Comfortable armchairs and plush sofas created private areas for one to sit in, whether to study or get lost in a book, as I had hoped to do today. Soft lighting cast a yellow glow over the room, creating pockets of color amid the vast expanse of knowledge that surrounded everyone who entered. Along the rear wall, the ancient building had been remodeled to add wall-to-wall windows overlooking the lush forest that lay beyond the library.

I could sit and stare into those trees for hours.

As I wandered through the twisty aisles, my fingers brushed along the spine of every tome I passed. Books of every genre imaginable lined the shelves, their spines worn with use. From timeless classics to the latest bestsellers, the library catered to all tastes and interests, ensuring there was a book for everyone to discover. There was a grand spiral staircase to the right of the main room that led to an upstairs section housing the library's collection of nonfiction and reference titles. On the second level, one could also find two tiny rooms. One was an office, and the other was the bathroom I'd been so desperate for the first time I'd visited.

My eyes scanned the nearest shelf, filled with book after book that I longed to read. The active librarian, Mrs. Matilda Sloan, was obsessive about keeping the selection in pristine condition, and I could always count on her to have the best books around. If you caught her in a good mood, she'd even pull together a reading list for you based on previous books you'd taken out from the library.

But it stood to reason she'd be so great with all things knowledge. Matilda Sloan was a sphinx, and her kind, while rare, were among the most intelligent paranormal creatures still in existence. In fact, you'd be hard-pressed to find a sphinx who didn't work a job focused on compiling large amounts of information. They were a brilliant bunch.

"Good morning, Lia," a cheerful voice called from somewhere off to my right.

Speak of the devil. I turned around and waved at Matilda behind the checkout counter. Today, the elderly woman wore a beehive of hair gathered in careful, tight curls above her head. She had four pens protruding from the large bun, with one more tucked behind her ear. Balancing on the curve of her long nose were wide, gold-rimmed glasses, her first line of defense when dealing with rowdy children. If you saw those babies slide down her nose, you'd best get quiet, or you'd find yourself on the receiving end of a stern scolding.

"Hi, Matilda," I chirped. "Anything new in?"

"I'd say!" The librarian pointed to a tall stack of books balancing precariously on the edge of her wide desk. "I'm still cataloging them, but if you stick around, I might have them ready before you leave."

"That's great. Not sure how long I'll be today, but I'll pop by before leaving."

"Anything particular you're here for?"

I shook my head. "No, I just needed to clear my head, as always."

"We had a few new mysteries come in last week if you want to give those a whirl. Second aisle on the left, you know the way."

I didn't have the heart to tell Matilda that, considering

all that had happened in my real life recently, a mystery was the last thing I wanted to read. Instead, I thanked her and then silently thanked the stars the librarian hated gossip. I didn't have the heart to talk about Polly's murder, and I was sure that news was circulating all over town by now.

One of the reasons I avoided the more popular gathering places was because of how deep everyone was in everyone else's business here in Bluejay Falls. It was cute until it hit close to home. Then, it was frustrating, to say the least.

Maneuvering the long way around the sitting area to avoid the mystery and thriller section, I ended up in young adult fiction and walked down the tight aisle. My hand grazed each book until I found the one I wanted. A paranormal romance about a young girl discovering she was a witch. The book was fairly short, and if I started now, I might've had a chance to read most of it before I had to leave today.

A loud crash a few aisles over made my heart leap into my throat, and I jumped back several inches from shock. Before I could rein it in, my vamp abilities took over, causing me to bite down on my tongue as my bones reformed.

The transformation, usually slow and agonizing, happened in a snap of the fingers. One second, I was holding the book in my hands, and the next, that book was on the floor, and I was flailing my tiny bat wings as I fought the pull of gravity. I groaned, and it came out in little chitters, because... bat.

"Sorry about that!" a deep voice came from the same direction as the loud racket. "I promise I'll fix it, Matilda!"

Was that Ryder?

Panic settled in my gut, and my eyes widened as I realized the detective was only a few aisles away. I thought I was alone here today, but of course, life had other plans. Not only was I not alone, but I was stuck in the same building as the one person in Bluejay I was desperately trying to avoid. The cherry on top of this hot dung sundae was that I was a bat.

Fang-tastic!

Not.

Heavy footsteps thudded against the wood floors, drawing nearer to where I flew, and my stress intensified to new heights. If I didn't get my act together and transform back immediately, I was going to have a huge problem on my wings... I mean, hands.

I spun around to find a place to hide, but the shelves in this aisle reached all the way to the ceiling and were fully stocked. There was nowhere to go but out the same way I'd come in, and from the sound of the approaching steps, that would have me flying right into the detective's face.

Bile rose in my little bat throat. I was trapped.

Closing my eyes tight, I concentrated on reforming, and by some small miracle, my body instantly obeyed. My limbs stretched out, and my body fell to the ground with a loud thud, landing on top of the dress I'd been wearing. The steps drew closer, and my heart hammered in my chest. Working at an inhuman speed, I threw myself into my dress and zipped it up, not bothering with undergarments.

Celebrate your freedom, girls! Grabbing the undergarments off the floor, I stuffed them into my purse.

I was still readjusting my dress when Detective Ryder made his grand entrance with all the subtlety of a runaway freight train. He turned the corner with such force that our bodies collided with a force more like a car collision than two people bumping into each other in a library. His broad chest met my side like a battering ram, sending me stumbling backward. My shoulder smacked against the bookshelf, triggering a cascade of paperbacks that fluttered to the floor like candy falling from a piñata.

Steadying myself, I discreetly checked the hem of my dress, determined to spare the detective from an inadvertent flash of my lady bits.

"Lia!" Ryder exclaimed when he saw me. "What are you doing here?"

I pointed to the books lying in tiny piles around us. "Oh, you know. Some light grocery shopping." The detective chuckled at my obvious sarcasm, the rich sound of it echoing through the aisles. "I didn't realize you were a fan of reading." The moment the words left my lips, I wished I could swallow them back.

Ryder quirked up an eyebrow. "Um, sure, yes. I actually come here often to clear my head."

"Me too. I'm sure you have a lot on your mind with all that's been going on."

"You can say that again." The detective leaned down to pick up a stack of books and place them back on the shelf.

As he reached for a second stack, his white shirt sleeve rolled up, revealing a small tattoo. A moon, if I wasn't mistaken.

After cramming the books back where they belonged, he straightened out to tower over me once more. "How have you been, by the way?"

Memories of the last few days and the long list of my scheming flashed through my mind. I tried to smile, but realizing it was likely more awkward than pleasant, I squatted to pick up the book I'd dropped when I shifted.

The back of my neck grew warm as I thought over what to say next, and I knew I was as red as a setting sun from the lies I was about to spew. Not wanting to complicate things further, I settled on answering the detective with the closest version of the truth I could muster.

"I've been on edge," I replied, tucking the book under my arm.

Ryder's full lips pressed together into a tight, thin line. "If I may offer some unsolicited advice?" When I nodded for him to continue, he said, "I've been doing this for some time now, and it never gets easier. If you're trying to forget about what happened to your client, it will only fester and drive you insane. The best way to move forward is to accept what happened, darkness and all."

Darker than you even know, I thought, not daring to say that out loud.

Instead, I looked Ryder straight in the eye and said, "I take it I'm no longer a prime suspect?"

He laughed again, and I tried not to think about the way my stomach skipped at the sound.

"I'm afraid that is yet to be determined," Ryder answered with a wink.

My idiotic stomach flipped again.

"Well, I suppose I'll leave you to your reading." His eyes flicked to the book tucked under my arm, and his lips twitched. "Enjoy the story."

I frowned, wrapping my fingers over the spine, suddenly embarrassed about my choice of novel. Why did Ryder even care what I read? So what if I liked a good teen love story? It wasn't a crime.

Whatever shame I may have had was quickly replaced by irritation, but I tamped it down, realizing it had been so long since I'd hung out with friends that it was more likely he meant the comment as good-natured teasing rather than an insult.

"Oh, since I have you here." Ryder paused, looking at me over his shoulder. "Can you ask your vet tech to come into the station?"

I stopped breathing.

"Bree?" I asked, knowing full well it wasn't the pixie the detective was interested in.

"No, the other one," he replied. "Justin Case. I have a few questions for him and would appreciate him coming in at his earliest convenience."

With that, he said his goodbyes and left me on my own

amid the sprawling shelves of books. Just the mention of Justin had my head spinning and my heart thundering against my chest. The aisle suddenly felt too tight, and I struggled to take a deep breath. I headed for one of the quiet reading nooks, where I could scrunch down in a chair and hide from the world.

Settling into one of the plush armchairs, I opened the book. I tried to ignore the pit that continued growing in my stomach, but I knew it wasn't going anywhere and that even a good love story couldn't distract me from the depressing thoughts weighing me down.

CHAPTER FOURTEEN

I ran the straw along the bottom of the box of Crimson Quench, sucking out every last drop. My head was spinning from having gone too many days without eating properly.

"One more?" Ashley asked.

At my nod, she slid a second juice across the counter. I caught it and hungrily stabbed the straw into the box.

"You really shouldn't go so long next time. I can see your fangs," she scolded with no real heat.

I could usually count on Ashley for a box of blood with a side of blunt truth. As one of the few paranormal business owners on Orfus Road, she ran The Roastery with an iron fist, and nothing escaped her notice. A paranormal couldn't cross the threshold unless they left their trouble at the door. It was an unspoken rule in the place and one Ashley took seriously. I once saw her toss a wolf on his butt because he'd treated a pixie with an attitude. The Roastery was as close as you could come to neutral ground in Bluejay Falls.

It was also one of my favorite places to visit when I was feeling out of sorts.

To help paranormals feel free to be themselves, Ashley hired a witch to cast a spell that deterred humans from wanting to come inside. Occasionally, an odd human would wander in, but that was rare. Ashley was a siren who didn't like the sordid history her kind shared with humanity, so it wasn't all that surprising that she preferred to avoid them. I assumed her opinions on how sirens treated humans had something to do with why she didn't have any family around, but I didn't press for details.

Minding your own business was another unspoken rule of the establishment.

I touched a finger to the tip of one fang and frowned. It had been years since I'd flashed my fangs without even realizing it.

"Here." Ashley passed me another box. "Can't have you advertising to every human on the street that Dracula exists. So, what has you up in knots?"

I looked behind her at the collection of nautical knots and ephemera on the bar shelves, tracing the intricate twists of rope and the weathered charm of maritime relics. The Roastery was—no surprise—a sea-themed wonderland, swallowing its customers in a watery fantasy from the moment they stepped inside.

The walls, painted a vibrant shade of blue reminiscent of the ocean's depths, boasted hand-painted waves that seemed to swell and crash halfway on the wall, bringing the sensation of being aboard a ship at sea. Each booth, decorated to resemble the deck of a wooden vessel, was a cozy hole to crawl into and relax while catching up on emails or reading a book.

Above my head, fishing nets draped the ceiling, their tangled webs adorned with starfish lamps that cast a warm glow in a shimmering shade of gold, making one feel like they were quite literally underwater. Even the menu went the extra mile to stay in character, with drinks like the Sea Salt Cream latte, the Tropical Storm Americano, and the Sunken Treasure Macchiato, all tasting exactly how they sounded, or so I was told.

Amid it all, Ashley stood proud, her passion for the sea reflected in every detail of the café's design.

I arched a brow at her pun, and she laughed. The sound vibrated the café, and a few of the male customers sat up a little straighter.

"Still got it," I said.

"Never gets old," the siren smirked. "Now, I believe you were about to tell me why you're on a hunger strike."

Sirens. They were like a hungry sea otter with an oyster when it came to sniffing out information. If you had something you wanted to keep a secret, you would be wise to avoid their kind unless you were up for an interrogation.

"I didn't starve myself on purpose if that's what you're thinking." I tapped my fang, then took another sip of Crimson Quench and blew out a relieved sigh when I felt the tooth retreat. "There are strange things going on in

Bluejay Falls, and I somehow managed to get in the middle of them."

"Really? You expect me to believe that? I know you too well, so try again." Ashley crossed her arms and narrowed her glowing blue eyes on me.

"Okay, fine!" I groaned, slumping further on the counter. "I shoved myself into the middle of things. But trust me, I don't have much of a choice. A person I'm close to is involved."

"Involved in a bad way?" Ashley asked, leaning her hip against the bar.

My chest constricted. "I'm not sure. He might be in trouble, or he might be *the* trouble. I'm trying to figure it out before an awful accusation gets pinned on an innocent person."

"You know, for a vamp, you've got a giant heart."

As Ashley stepped to the left to refill a dragon shifter's coffee cup, the front door swung open. My nose twitched as a familiar scent blew inside, and I spun around on the creaky bar stool to face the entrance. Barely able to squeeze through the frame, Skeeter contorted his large body to make it fit through the door. Once inside, his serious gaze rolled over the café, looking for a spot to sit.

When he spotted me, his eyes lit up, and he strode toward me. "Lia! Good to see you again." He pointed to his no longer swollen jaw. "You're a miracle worker."

I patted the empty seat next to me and waited for Skeeter to sit down. "Glad to hear you're feeling better. If you have any more trouble, just give me a call."

"Will do."

Perusing the chalkboard menu, Skeeter settled for a double shot espresso, patiently sitting while Ashley got it ready. The smell of freshly brewed coffee wafted through the café, and my stomach turned. My body was still recovering from the lack of sustenance. I sipped the rest of my Crimson Quench and waited for it to settle before turning back to Skeeter.

"I meant to call you this morning to thank you, by the way," I told the troll. "For helping me out with the notebook."

"Of course! I nearly forgot." Skeeter reached into his back pocket and pulled out a small notebook.

He leafed through it, spreading it wide on the counter between us. I craned my neck to peer over his wide shoulders.

"Are those the numbers from the book?" I asked.

"Yep!" Seeing my amazement at his memorization skills, Skeeter tapped his forehead and said, "Photographic memory. I wrote them down as soon as the sedatives wore off. I wanted to see if I could figure anything else out that might help you."

"Did you?"

A mischievous glimmer sparked in Skeeter's eyes. "Sure did. I wasn't convinced at first, but after further examination, I realized what was bothering me about the last set of numbers."

He flipped a page in the notebook and pointed to a long

string of random code. "These differ from the rest, but I couldn't put my finger on why."

"Huh," I whispered.

Now that he had pointed it out, I could see what he meant. The numbers Skeeter pointed to did not match the other sequences. For one, it was longer. Then, there were the random commas in between them. The troll was right—they didn't match.

I chewed my lip and looked up at him. "Any chance you know what they mean?"

The troll reached into his jacket for his cell phone, tapping a few keys before turning it toward me. On the screen was a map I recognized instantly.

"Is that...?"

"The marina," Skeeter agreed. "The numbers are a location." He circled a small section on the map with a fingernail. "Right here, to be exact."

Studying the area, I creased my brow in concentration and tried to fit the pieces of the puzzle together. Dates for past robberies and a location in the marina. What was Polly doing with these? Why were they so important that she'd taken the time to hide them? And how was Justin involved?

I was completely stumped.

Taking another look at the map, I nudged Skeeter's side. "Feel like taking a drive to the water?"

The troll was already standing. "I thought you'd never ask."

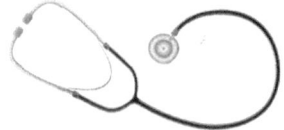

WE REACHED the docks in record time, mostly thanks to Skeeter, who insisted he drive. On the way over, he ran two stoplights, traveled double the speed limit, and nearly took out his side mirror with a street sign. I had to fight the urge to transform into a bat and dart out the window every couple of miles.

When the car finally stopped, I peeled my white-knuckled hand away from the overhead bar and rubbed the throbbing muscles in my legs where I'd stayed tense the entire ride. Skeeter, however, was happy as a clam and skipped the entire way from the dock's parking lot down to the water. I followed slowly behind him on rubbery limbs.

The Bluejay Falls docks were essentially a barely used shipping yard. A few of the locals still used it to tie off their boats, but for the most part, the place was abandoned. Empty wrappers and empty beer cans were strewn around one overflowing garbage can, and every few feet, there were dark, wet stains on the pavement. I had no idea what the stains were, and I didn't want to find out.

The smell of the water surrounded us as we marched up the rickety boardwalk toward the location marker Skeeter had shown me on the map. A small boat rocked against the wooden planks, the sound mimicking our steps. The sea was grumpy today.

"It should be just around the corner." Skeeter veered off

the boardwalk toward the industrial buildings that were tightly squeezed together off to our right.

Most of them were old storage units for the businesses that used to run along the dock back when this place was still operational, but now there were only empty lots where those businesses had once stood. As far as I knew, the remaining buildings were either abandoned or barely used —which seemed to be confirmed by the boarded-up windows and doors.

Trailing after Skeeter, I watched as he disappeared between two especially decrepit-looking units and rushed to catch up.

"Are you sure it's here?" I called out.

No answer.

Panic crawled up my body, and I bolted forward, my shoulders scraping against the rough walls of the buildings on either side of me. *How did Skeeter even fit through here?*

My footsteps echoed through the narrow space, pounding in my eardrums. For the first time in my entire life, I understood what it meant to feel claustrophobic. Ahead of me, a sliver of light lit the way. I ran toward it at the speed of light. Emerging on the other side, I skidded to a stop an inch away from colliding with Skeeter's massive back.

He turned around to see what the commotion was, then shot me a confused look.

As I bent over to catch a breath, Skeeter pointed to a two-story warehouse ahead of us. "It's that place."

"Are you sure? It doesn't look very lively," I wheezed, still trying to regulate my breathing.

Much like the rest of the surrounding buildings, the warehouse appeared to have been out of use for quite some time. Wooden planks covered every window, and there were broken shards of glass covering the perimeter of the building. They sparkled in the glimmer of the sun above us, giving the overgrown weeds jutting out of the cracked concrete lot a freshly watered look.

Beside me, Skeeter grunted under his breath. "The numbers never lie."

He took the lead as we made our way to what had once been the front entrance. However, we could have simply gone through any of the busted-out openings created by either time, weather, or kids messing around. I stepped into a mud puddle as we crossed into the warehouse, and my foot sank several inches into a thick layer of mud. Clenching my jaw, I pulled my shoe free and tried not to think about my wet sock for the rest of the walk.

I really, really hated wet socks.

The deeper into the warehouse we journeyed, the more this trip felt like a dead end. The interior of the building had been gutted, and there wasn't so much as a single shelf left around. Ivy grew up the walls and reached out toward the second story, which didn't seem to be structurally safe at all. If I tilted my head enough, I could see through the broken second-floor beams all the way to the roof. As my gaze drifted around the stark interior, I spotted a staircase, but even that seemed unusable thanks to the number of planks it was missing.

"Let's not go in too much farther," I whispered, scooting closer to Skeeter. "I don't think it's safe."

"It's not as bad as it looks. See?" The troll leaned his hand on a wall and winced when it crumpled under his weight, letting sunshine stream into the building's dusty interior.

He quickly removed his hand and hurried to change the subject. "You never told me where you got the notebook. It might help me figure out why the numbers led us here."

I sighed. "Trust me, it's better you don't know. I'm starting to think this entire thing was nothing more than the overactive imagination of a lonely woman."

Giving the warehouse one last look, I turned on my heel and headed back the way we'd come. "We should get out of here before the whole thing collapses on our heads."

As we walked back into the warm sunshine, I kept sneaking glances over my shoulder. Perhaps what I'd told Skeeter was true, and Polly hadn't been in her right mind. For all I knew, she had a fascination with crime, and the notebook was nothing more than her obsession coming to light. Because no matter how I spun this, I had trouble picturing the parrot owner as some sort of criminal mastermind.

Then again, I also couldn't picture Justin killing her over an argument. No wonder the police were so keen on keeping me in town so they could ask me more questions. This case made absolutely zero sense.

Putting Polly's murder out of my mind for the time being, I concentrated on Justin and how to find him. It was too early to call the cops and report him missing, especially since I wasn't his next of kin. I was his boss, but unless he missed more than one shift, I doubted the cops would even take my concerns seriously.

And I couldn't exactly tell the cops about the traces of his presence I'd found at Polly's without also explaining what I'd been doing there. As far as the police were concerned, it would have been better if they had never known I had been there.

Next of kin...

My eyes widened as I recalled Justin's benefits application. If I couldn't report him missing to the police without raising suspicion, maybe someone else could... someone related to Justin.

Someone whose phone number I had back at the clinic.

CHAPTER FIFTEEN

I t was late in the day by the time I got a hold of Justin's sister, and we had made plans to meet. I'd been hoping to spend my first day off in months binging crime shows and becoming one with the couch, but that was not in the cards. Instead, I found myself staring at a garish bouquet of mismatched flowers on a dinner table that had seen better days.

Dina's Diner was a short drive from the clinic, but it felt like a world away. Gone was the charm of our quaint street, with its bustle of people with smiling faces. The few patrons gracing the grease-covered establishment wouldn't know a smile if it hit them in the face.

My belly rolled as I watched a man dump four table-spoons of sugar into his coffee cup. The scent of burning bacon clogged the air, and my nausea intensified. I dug my nails into the torn bench seat cover for dear life, hoping I wouldn't vamp out in this dump.

"Can I take your order?" a woman asked, smacking the gum she was chewing between words.

I smiled. "Not yet. I'm waiting for someone."

"All righty then." The woman turned, then paused and called over her shoulder, "Specials are on the back of the menu."

I flipped the ripped page in front of me, its sticky film coating catching the dim light filtering through the dusty windows. Pretending to read the selections, I shifted my weight slightly, keeping my senses alert as I darted glances at the dirty front door.

It was ten minutes past the time we'd agreed to meet, and I was starting to think she might not show up. A sense of restlessness gnawed at my insides as I tried to figure out what my next step should be. Behind me, someone began coughing up a lung, and I was two seconds away from rushing out of the restaurant when the front door swung open. It was difficult to see through the smudged hand-print-covered glass, but I knew it was her.

Bess Case poked her long nose into the diner and took in the interior with a quick sweep of her sharp eyes. Her high cheekbones were painted a bright shade of apricot, and when she brushed the wavy mane of dark hair away from her face, the resemblance to Justin was unmistakable. If I didn't know better, I'd think they were twins.

Putting the menu down, I waved meekly and waited until she hovered over the booth to say hello.

Bess sucked in a breath through the gap between her two front teeth. "You said you wanted to talk about Justin?"

Straight to the point, then. Got it.

I pointed to the empty bench across from me, and Bess curled her lip before reluctantly lowering herself onto the seat. Her feet tapped a rhythm under the table, and she kept glancing at the clock above the serving station. It was no secret this was the last place she wanted to be.

Straightening my shoulders, I slid the menu across the table to her. "Do you want a coffee? On me."

"I'd like to know what you want with my brother," she said bitterly. "And then I'd like to leave."

Wowza. And I thought Justin could be on the blunt, almost rude side. My vet tech was never one for friendly conversation, but at least he had the decency to hide it behind a wide smile and a few welcoming words. Bess was all sharp edges and pointed teeth, a stick of a woman who could cut you in half with a simple look. Maybe this meeting wasn't the smartest idea.

If I was way off base with my suspicions, and it turned out Justin was fine, I'd surely never hear the end of it once Bess relayed the story. No doubt she'd tell him how his unhinged boss had cornered her in a filthy diner when she was in a hurry to leave.

My heart beat a little faster. *But what if he's in trouble?*

Inhaling, I calmed my rising nerves and tried reasoning with her. Worst-case scenario, I'd compel her, but I really preferred to go a day without using my vamp abilities. Ever since Polly had shown up at the clinic, I found that was getting harder and harder to do.

"I'll make this quick, I promise," I told Bess. "When was the last time you spoke to Justin?"

She quirked one brow in my direction. "Is he in some sort of trouble?"

"Not at all." I tried to sound reassuring. "Something came up with a client he handled, and I can't seem to reach him. I was hoping you might be able to help out."

"Let me get this straight. You called me over here because of a work thing that doesn't appear to be remotely urgent. Can't you ask him next shift?"

I swallowed the lump in my throat. "I want to handle it sooner rather than later, and I have to admit, I'm getting a bit worried about not being able to reach your brother."

Footsteps shuffled next to us as the server from earlier returned to the table. She'd swapped the gum for a bright green lollipop that she didn't bother spitting out before asking us if we were ready to order. I got the distinct feeling the server would ask us to leave unless we ordered something.

Scanning the menu, I settled on a cup of coffee, which I obviously wouldn't drink, and waited for Bess to order. Surprisingly, she got a full all-day breakfast with a side of fries. It seemed like a lot of food for someone who was in such a hurry, but I was glad I would at least have her ear until the end of the meal.

Relaxing into the seat, I gave her a friendly smile. "In case I didn't mention it before, I'm very grateful you came all the way out here to talk to me. I wouldn't have asked if I didn't think it was important."

Bess barked out a laugh.

"Sorry, do you think it's funny that your brother might be missing?" I asked, unable to help myself.

The question earned me another solid laugh. "Justin isn't missing."

"So you have spoken to him recently?"

Bess shrugged. "Recent enough. But believe me when I tell you, if Justin isn't picking up his phone, it's for a reason."

My brow creased. "What type of reason?"

"Not to sound rude, but why do you care so much? Last I heard, Justin wasn't even that great at his job."

Yikes. Where was Bess getting her information from? It sounded like she didn't know her brother at all. One thing I always admired about Justin was how dedicated he was to the job. Sure, he complained more than Bree and rarely showed up outside his scheduled shifts, but the man knew his animals and always treated them with a gentleness I admired.

A thought that had been lurking in the back of my mind leaped to the forefront. Why had Justin been so eager to help me out when Polly called? I'd asked him to come in multiple times before when we were swamped, and he almost always had a reason not to. Yet when I told him about receiving an emergency call for a parrot named Elvis, he practically jumped at the chance to help. He'd even shown up at a reasonable time.

The idea bothered me, and I couldn't quite put my finger on why.

Tearing myself away from my inner musings, I focused back on Bess. "Justin is one of my best employees," I corrected her.

"He'd have to be," she said. "You pay the bills."

A tray slid on the table between us as the server dropped off my coffee and Bess's food. She did so without even looking at either of us, which was both infuriating and impressive. I'd imagine you'd have to grow a thicker skin to work in this place, considering the clientele. My eyes flicked sideways to the table next to ours, where the man I saw earlier had fallen asleep with his face in a stack of pancakes.

The next time I felt like complaining about the clinic, I'd think twice. It was heaven compared to working here.

Shaking my head, I watched Bess take a massive bite out of her jelly-smeared toast and waited until she swallowed.

"I didn't get the impression that Justin was a vet tech for the money." Memories of his apartment flashed before me. "Though I have to admit, I was impressed by his stunning apartment building."

"Don't let appearances fool you," Bess said mid-chew. "He got the apartment after our parents died. I was living in Europe at the time, and Justin was always terrible with money, so I let him have it. And I'll have you know he took it without giving me so much as a thank you. Sure enough, when I returned and needed help to get back on my feet, Justin couldn't be bothered."

"Oh. I had no idea," I murmured. It made more sense

now how Justin could afford the place on a vet tech's salary. "I'm sorry about your parents."

Bess bit into a piece of bacon like a feral creature. "Don't be. They were terrible people. Mom was never around, and Dad… Well, Dad is the reason Justin has his little problem now."

My pulse spiked.

"Problem?" I asked, leaning forward so aggressively, the edge of the table pressed hard against my sternum.

"His, you know"—she made a money motion with her index and thumb—"gambling problem."

His what? Since when did Justin have a gambling problem, and how did I not know about it when I hired him? At the very least, Bree should have had an idea if there was an issue since that girl's hobby was tracking everyone's business. To say I was shocked would have been an understatement. My jaw practically hit the table. This was the last thing I'd expected her to say.

Across from me, Bess's cheeks reddened. "I take it you didn't know. Listen, I probably shouldn't have mentioned it. I'm sure he's not as bad as he used to be, but it would explain why he's AWOL. Justin tends to go off the radar when he's deep in it, which is why I don't think there's anything to worry about."

"H-How bad does he get?" I stuttered. "Is Justin having financial problems?"

Shaking her head, Bess polished off another bacon slice without chewing. "We're all having financial problems, aren't we? He can become pretty desperate. Even borrowed money from my boyfriend once that he has yet to pay back. But what can you do? Family and all that bullcrap."

She shoved a few fries in her mouth and glanced back at the clock. "Anyhow, I'd wait it out if I were you. He'll show up sooner or later. Or just go ahead and fire him. You probably can't do any worse. I have a date I'm late for." Sliding the plate to the side, she waved the server over, saying, "It's on the big boss here."

Without giving me a chance to say another word, Bess stood and sauntered away. I sat staring at the door long after she left, absolutely baffled by the conversation.

Had she been exaggerating? Somehow, I didn't think so. And if she'd told me the truth, it meant the person I'd hired wasn't who I thought he was.

Could Justin have been desperate enough for money that he was willing to kill over it? Perhaps he'd decided to rob a robber? It was a motive that would make sense, and no matter how much I wanted to dismiss it, a part of me felt compelled to follow the theory... like an itch I had to scratch.

If Polly Ester had been responsible for the robberies in Bluejay Falls, she'd likely have had untraceable cash stashed in her house. I didn't know Justin extremely well, but if I had a gambling addiction, I imagined Polly would make an excellent target. After all, a criminal couldn't exactly call the cops on you if you reverse Uno'd their stolen loot.

Especially not if they were dead.

My skin crawled, and I rubbed my hands down my arms as though warding off a chill.

I paid the bill and headed out of the diner. The smell of bacon had seeped into my clothes, and I gagged in my mouth the entire way across the parking lot.

Rubbing my temples, I climbed into the driver's side and rested my forehead on the steering wheel. I didn't even realize I'd drifted off until a vibration in my jacket pocket jarred me awake, and I jerked back so hard I nearly gave myself whiplash.

Squinting at the Caller ID and recognizing the name, I answered it without a second thought. "Bree?"

"Sorry to do this, but you need to come in."

The urgency in my tech's voice had me panicked. "What happened?"

"It's Justin," she said. "He didn't come in for his shift."

A loud screech sounded on the other line, followed by a howl.

Even though both Bree and Justin were licensed veterinarian technicians, they couldn't provide medical care to patients without a vet on the premises. On my night off, the appointments were routine things like applying fresh dressings, nail trims, weight checks, and picking up prescription refills. However, there were still too many appointments for Bree to handle alone.

I popped the phone into a stand on the dash and put it on speaker. "Did you try calling him?"

"Sure did. Five times." Bree's answer was followed by

another howl. "No answer. I'm really sorry to call you on your night off, but it's a zoo over here. Quite literally."

Chuckling, I reversed out of the parking spot and hit the road. "Don't worry about it. I'll be there soon. I just have to stop by the house to pick up the children."

"See you, Byrd, and Elvis in a bit," Bree breathed in relief. "And thank you! I know it's your only night off."

Hanging up, I let Bree get back to wrangling whatever chaos had descended on the clinic. I stepped on the gas and sped home. It took less than ten minutes to gather Byrd and Elvis, both of whom were more than happy to be out of the house and ready for a change of scenery.

Elvis chatted the entire way there, throwing in a random mention of a star again. He was on a real astronomy kick lately.

Whatever expectations I had walking into the clinic were shattered upon entrance. My mouth gaped as I took in the scene in the waiting room, unable to figure out where to start.

A massive white owl was perched on the reception desk, its talons tearing up the printer paper with obvious malice. Off to its right, a black lab barked at the paper-hating owl and attempted to jump at it while both owners tried to intercept. A yellow lab had its nose deep in a bag of doggy treats it had nabbed from the display shelf and ripped open.

As I turned in a slow circle, I found a hedgehog huddled in its owner's scarf just outside one of the exam rooms, and a man with a lizard sticking out of his pocket sat in a chair opposite her.

Since I couldn't see Bree anywhere, I assumed she had taken one of the paranormal patients into the back room and away from our human clients' curious gazes.

"Hi, everyone," I told the room. "Let's get you all situated."

Placing the inquisitive labradors in a room away from the chaotic excitement of the waiting room helped to lower their excitement, which gave me enough time to deposit Elvis's cage in the kitchen and drop Byrd off in his favorite hiding spot under the sink.

Working as fast as possible, I breezed through the appointments, switching out with Bree when a couple of our walk-in patients ended up needing more serious medical care. It took us the better part of three hours to clear everyone out, and in the end, we were both slick with sweat and slightly breathless.

I waved goodbye to a witch and her owl familiar and watched them scurry down the street as I locked the door shut behind them. Leaning back against the door, I caught Bree's eyes as she sagged into a waiting room chair, exhausted.

"That was a lot." I covered my mouth to hide a yawn.

"You're telling me!" she exclaimed. "Bill the werewolf needs a rabies shot, by the way. I put him on the schedule for tomorrow."

"Sounds good." Pushing away from the door, I walked past her and bent to pick up the shredded paper under the desk, tossing it into the trash.

It was about an hour before we were technically closing,

but after the last few appointments, Bree and I agreed to call it a night a little earlier.

I headed down the hallway to the kitchen, glancing back at her over my shoulder. "I'm going to try Justin again."

"Tell him he owes us big time!"

Chuckling, I left her to rest and made my way to the rear of the clinic. When I neared, I noticed the back door stood slightly ajar.

The werewolf must have left it open when he left tonight. I started for it, pausing when another object caught my attention.

Sitting on the kitchen counter was Elvis's cage.

It was empty.

"No, no, no!" I shouted, running for the door.

The sound of wings flapping rushed up behind me as Byrd came out of his hiding spot to see what the commotion was. The curious bat followed me outside, and we burst into the dark back alley. My eyes took a second to adjust to the low light, and then I moved forward to inspect the alley. A loud squawk broke the eerie silence. My gaze flicked to the dumpster that sat at the back of the dead-end alley. I let out a shuddering breath and felt hot tears prick my eyes.

Perched atop the smelly metal can was Elvis. His feathers ruffled, and his beak tapped away at the lid of the dumpster.

"Elvis!" I whispered, not wanting to spook him into taking flight. "What are you doing out here? You almost gave me a heart attack."

Behind me, hanging upside from the eaves, Byrd chit-tered in agreement.

I slowly walked toward the parrot, trying my best not to make any sudden moves. My shoe crushed an empty soda can, and I winced when the sound echoed down the alley. A few steps away from me, Elvis's head shot up, peering hard in my direction.

"Easy…"

Examining me for another few seconds, Elvis lost his interest and went back to tapping. *Why is he so fascinated by a trash bin?*

One shaky step at a time, I drew nearer the parrot. When I finally closed in on him, I had to skirt around the dump-ster to get a better angle so I could coax the feathery escape artist off the top. Holding my breath to avoid inhaling the stench of garbage that intensified with every step I took, I reached up toward Elvis.

A glimmer of light from just behind the bin caught my attention, and I stopped what I was doing to glance down. For a moment, time seemed to be suspended, and the next, everything happened all at once.

As my gaze went to the light, I stared unblinking at the ground behind the dumpster while Elvis let out another ear-drum-shattering squawk. The sound caused Byrd to drop from the eaves, and he came flapping to my side with all the speed and elegance of a drunk raccoon in a pottery shop. Byrd slammed into the dumpster's metal side, sending vibrations through the metal that startled Elvis, and he took flight, heading down the alley and back inside the clinic.

In the commotion exploding around me, I lost my balance and stumbled backward, my shoulders smashing into the adjacent wall. A dull pain shot down my body, but I barely registered it because my attention was fully focused on the shattered screen of the cell phone that lay on the ground.

Despite the glass being badly cracked, the phone still worked, and its light illuminated the dark space between the dumpster and the wall.

In that tight space lay a large mass that didn't belong there.

My eyes widened as I made out the shape of a lifeless body that lay on the ground. There was no mistaking who it was, and I tried to scream, only to have it get caught in my throat where it threatened to suffocate me.

Now I knew why Justin hadn't shown up for work tonight and why we hadn't been able to get a hold of him.

Hot tears blurred my eyes, and the edges of my vision turned dark as my legs gave out, sending me collapsing to the ground in a heap.

My vet tech was dead.

CHAPTER SIXTEEN

Yellow tape adorned the back alley of the clinic in dizzying, zigzagging patterns. It was a stark contrast to the usual darkness of the alley, turning it both intriguing and foreboding at the same time. If it wasn't for the grim reality it represented, I might have mistaken this for a meticulously designed movie set for a crime show.

I pulled the scratchy blanket tighter around my shoulders, the coarse fabric a pathetic attempt at warding off the chill of the night. Though uncomfortable against my skin, it helped a bit to dispel the cold that was seeping through my clothes and into my bones. Sitting on the low steps of the clinic's rear exit, I remained a silent observer while the police worked.

Before me, they continued carefully examining Justin's lifeless body. Every movement of their gloved hands on his pale skin felt like another twist of the knife in my gut, a reminder of the reality of what had happened.

Elvis's cage sat on the ground beside me, and for the first time since I'd met him, he was utterly silent.

A cluster of officers had gathered near the dumpster, their hushed murmurs sending shivers down my spine. My heart lodged in my throat as Ryder walked the length of the alley toward them, preparing to interrupt whatever was going on.

In the glow of the bright lights the police had set up in the alley, his gaze found mine, freezing me in place as though I were one of those expensive ice sculptures that were popular at stuffy events and over-the-top weddings.

Please don't come over here.

He held up a finger to let me know he'd deal with me momentarily. Of course he would. I gathered up the blanket tighter at my neck and wondered if I might suffocate myself before Ryder approached.

"Here." Bree brandished a travel coffee mug in front of my face. "You need to eat."

I looked up at her from my blanket noose and whispered, "I can't drink that."

"Just take it," the vet tech said, lowering herself to sit beside me. "I emptied a Crimson Quench into it."

Accepting the drink, I unenthusiastically sipped on it, lost in the thoughts swirling in my head. I couldn't believe Justin was dead. All this time, I was running around trying to pin Polly's murder on him, and the poor guy wasn't even breathing. I felt like the worst boss in the history of employ-ment. Worse, I felt like a horrible person.

What kind of vampire was I? There had been a dead body literally feet away from my doorstep, and I hadn't even smelled it. Granted, the stench of garbage did a good job of masking it. Otherwise, I would've noticed it instantly.

I took another sip, wiping my lips for any stains that would imply I wasn't drinking any old regular coffee. "What do you think happened to him?"

"No clue," Bree said, shrugging. "At least now we know where he's been. Sorry, I don't do well with death. If I get too awkward, just tell me to leave, okay?"

"It's fine. Have the police talked to you yet?"

She shook her head, her gaze landing on Ryder. "That guy said to stick around for a while, but that's about it. Although I wouldn't mind having a chat with him. Yum." Her eyes widened, and even in the dim light, I could see the blush painting her cheeks. "Again, sorry. Death. Yikes."

I wasn't sure what made me more uncomfortable—Bree's word vomit or the fact that she found Ryder attrac-tive. Eyes flicking to the detective, I ground my teeth. He was easy on the eyes, but the obnoxious way in which he carried himself was a huge turnoff.

Although, I could be biased because of the whole thing where he was trying to pin a murder on me. Either way, I couldn't think of Ryder as anything but a problem. One that made me nervous about being around him for any length of time.

On the ground, Elvis echoed a string of incoherent nonsense.

"I can take him inside if you want," Bree offered.

Nodding, I thanked her as I stretched my legs out in front of me. The sun was starting to peek over the horizon, casting shades of gold and red into the alley. If it wasn't for the grim scene before me, it would have been pretty. Until that moment, I hadn't realized how quiet and isolated it was behind the clinic.

My breath hitched.

What was Justin doing back here, anyway?

"Miss Pane? A few words, please."

My jaw clamped shut, biting my tongue in the process. I winced at the sharp pain and the taste of iron that filled my mouth. Reluctantly, I tilted my head back to look up at the detective towering over me.

Here we go again.

Forcing a smile, I stood, the blanket falling half off my shoulder. "Sure. Do you want to go inside?"

Ryder raised his nose in the air, then jerked his head toward the door and followed me into the clinic. As we marched down the hallway toward one of the examination rooms, I noticed Bree's eyes tracking our every move. She mouthed silent words I couldn't understand, though if it was anything like the conversation I had with her before, maybe it was for the best.

I opened the door and motioned for the detective to come inside. As he stepped over the threshold, his gaze flicked around the room, noting the framed pictures of happy pets on the walls and the shelves lined with medical supplies. Ryder was out of his element, and I fought a small grin as he shrunk a little.

How the tables have turned, buddy.

Ryder opened his mouth to speak, but I held up a hand to stop him. "Look, before we do this again, I need you to know that I had nothing to do with what happened to Justin. I was actually trying to find him. You can ask his neighbor and his sister. They'll vouch for me."

"You can relax, Miss Pane. I don't think you killed your vet tech." His brow furrowed. "Wait. When were you at Mr. Case's apartment building?"

I swallowed the lump in my throat. "Um, yesterday, I guess? Sorry, the days tend to blur together when you work night shifts."

"You must have missed us," Ryder said. "We were there the same day following a lead. Why do you work so many night shifts?"

"It makes sense for what we do. Not a lot of vets around these parts are open late. Some owners can't make it to appointments during regular business hours. And animals have emergencies too, you know."

The detective smirked. "Trust me, I know. My ex had a French bulldog that was incredibly accident-prone. It would have been nice to have somewhere like your clinic nearby." He raked his fingers through his hair, tousling it out of place. "Benny is still a walking disaster. You might hear from us soon."

"You kept the dog?"

"Definitely," Ryder replied. "Always liked him better than the ex. So tell me about what happened here tonight."

I sighed. The weight of the night was finally catching up to me, and I knew that if I didn't get through it soon, I'd fall apart right here in the examination room. Justin and I weren't close. We weren't friends, but finding him dead and seeing him lying there... was too much.

If I thought what happened with Polly was bad, this was a million times worse. It didn't help that I had Bree to think about, though she handled it pretty well. Maybe even better than me.

I stifled the overwhelming grief I felt for Justin and faced the detective head-on. "After the last appointment, I went to check on Elvis, but he was gone. The back door was open, so naturally, I assumed he'd escaped. I rushed over there as quickly as possible, and sure enough, he was on top of the dumpster."

I left the part about the bat out because I didn't have it in me to explain why he was casually living in the clinic rent-free. "Anyway, Elvis wouldn't come down. I tried to get a better angle so I could reach him. That's when I saw Justin. I called the police right away."

Leaning on the table in the corner, Ryder noted what I said in a small notebook, his eyes flicking between me and the book. "To confirm, Elvis is Polly Ester's parrot, correct?"

I nodded.

"Can you describe what you saw when you first realized it was Mr. Case behind the dumpster?"

"N-Not much," I stuttered. "As I mentioned, once I realized what happened, I called you immediately and went to wait inside. I didn't want to be... out there. Do you know what happened to Justin? No one has told me anything."

Not answering my question, the detective scribbled down words in the notebook again and underlined them twice. "Did you see any blood on the scene?"

"Blood?" I asked, baffled. I didn't recall seeing or smelling anything of the kind. But again, the dumpster was full, and it wasn't exactly a French perfumery out there.

"I can't tell you much about an ongoing investigation." Ryder clicked his pen. "I can tell you it appears Mr. Case was murdered, and from what we can tell, he was dragged behind the dumpster post mortem. It was as though he was magically deposited there."

My pulse hammered in my veins so hard I thought I might faint. The rational part of me knew the detective didn't mean real magic since he was human, but now that the idea was out there, my brain wouldn't let it go. *How did Justin end up behind the dumpster?*

A thought ran laps in my mind, and I finally caught it, turning it this way and that until it made sense.

"Justin had a shift tonight he didn't show up for," I told the detective. "Do you think the killer was waiting for Justin and killed him when he arrived for work?"

"It's possible. Was Mr. Case known for using the alley entrance to come to work?"

"Not really," I admitted, chewing my lip.

"All right. It gives us a possible timeline, at least." He rubbed the nape of his neck. "You mentioned going to the victim's apartment and that you talked with his sister. Was there a reason for you to be worried about Mr. Case's whereabouts?"

Whelp. There was no way to explain this without telling him about the notebook and the random leads Skeeter and I had been following.

Coming clean was the right choice.

I knew it was a smart decision.

But instead of telling Ryder about all of it, I only nodded like an imbecile. "I called him a few times, and he didn't reply. It made me worry. I figured I should check on him."

My throat was suddenly dry. "Shoot! Has anyone told his sister yet?"

"She's meeting me at the station in an hour," Ryder said. "Is there anything else you can think of that might help us understand what happened tonight? Did Justin have any enemies? Did you see him act differently lately?"

I pressed my lips into a thin line. "Honestly, not that I noticed. He was always reserved, and our relationship was strictly business. Justin was good at what he did, and that was all that mattered to me. He cared about our patients." My breath wavered. "I can't believe he's gone."

Brain in overdrive, I tried to think of how I could mention finding Justin's gum in Polly's backyard without getting myself arrested. While my dislike of Ryder had softened, I still didn't trust him not to blame the entire thing on me. It seemed I had some long-buried issues with authority I needed to deal with in the future.

You learn new information about yourself every day. Go figure.

Sucking in a quick breath, I said, "I mentioned this before, but I think it might be an important piece to this puzzle. Justin seemed almost eager to come in when I mentioned Elvis's name, and he wasn't a fan of coming in after hours. But then he had a run-in with Polly over some bloodwork for Elvis when she came in. I thought nothing of it then, but now, with both of them dead... It seems odd. Looking back, it was almost like they were fighting over something else, like maybe they'd met before, but I could be wrong."

"So you think the two deaths could be related?"

"Possibly," I whispered.

Ryder straightened his back out, suddenly appearing much taller. "I'd have to agree. It's worth looking into, at least."

Flipping the notebook shut, he tucked it back into his jeans pocket. I stepped aside to let him through the door, then followed him outside. Ryder stopped at the back door, standing in the doorway, looking almost ominous as he pinned his gaze on me, his body backlit by the rising sun.

"If you think of anything else," he said, handing me a card, "call me. Anytime."

"Are you working the robberies?" I blurted out before I could stop myself.

Shut up, Lia! You're becoming as talkative as Elvis!

Ryder's eyebrow twitched. "My team is. Why?"

"No specific reason," I lied... badly. "Seems this town

isn't what it used to be. It would be good if you could find whoever is responsible and make us all feel a little safer again."

"We're trying our best, Miss Pane," Ryder sighed, and I believed him. "There are multiple jurisdictions involved since the crimes were committed in several towns. And without many clues, it's hard to find the connections. But trust me, it is our top priority aside from these homicides. There is no reason for you to feel unsafe in Bluejay Falls."

On instinct, my eyes looked past him to the dumpster, where two men were wheeling a stretcher with a white sheet shaped like my vet tech away.

From the corner of my vision, I saw Ryder wince. "I'm going to head inside and speak with your other vet tech now, but feel free to call me anytime, Miss Pane."

As he turned on his heel and marched off, I stared unseeing into the alley. My heart beat wildly in my ribcage, and I found it hard to take a full breath. Now that the police were almost finished, there were a few things I needed to handle.

First, I needed to close the clinic down for a short while. I knew it would be a problem for some of my patients, but there was no way Bree or I were in any shape to work. We needed a few days to wrap our heads around what happened.

I assumed there'd be a funeral soon as well.

And I should check in with Justin's sister later, too.

All I wanted was to go home and sleep for days. No, that wasn't true. What I wanted more than anything was to wake up from this nightmare. Who would have thought a vampire would be caught up in so much death? Our kind worked hard to put that stereotype behind us, and here I was, trailing death in my wake like it was the new black.

A vibration in my back pocket had me yelping and grabbing my chest. Pulling out my phone, I saw a familiar number and Skeeter's face on the screen. I tapped the notification and read his message, my mouth gaping.

You have got to be kidding me.

CHAPTER SEVENTEEN

"Are you absolutely sure?" I asked Skeeter for the fourth time, clutching my cell phone to my ear.

Skeeter snorted. "Yes, Lia. I'm absolutely sure. The warehouse in Polly's book belongs to Tim Burr, who owns the Grab 'n Go near her home."

I knew when it came to finding out information no one was better at it than a troll, and no troll was better at it than Skeeter. That man could figure out your deepest, darkest secrets with access to the internet and enough free time on his hands.

But it was still hard to believe.

"Okay, thanks for letting me know, Skeeter." We said our goodbyes, and I jumped into action.

Which is how I found myself sucking down two blood juice boxes in a row and pushing my tired eyes wide open as I marched toward the yellow convenience store at the

SEDONA JADE & AMY STAKE

end of Flytrap Lane. Hey, I never said I was a patient woman.

The store appeared on the horizon, and my breath caught in my chest. Why would Polly note a warehouse that belonged to a shop owner on her street? And why layer it in codes in the notebook to hide it?

The deeper I got into this mess, the less I understood what was happening. *I should really cut my losses and give the notebook to the police.*

An image of me in cuffs for withholding evidence and interfering with an active investigation flashed before me. *Ugh! How did I get myself into this mess?*

Oh yes, Justin. My vet tech had something to do with all of it, and I needed to find out what happened before both our names got dragged through the mud.

My muscles ached as I picked up the pace until I was practically jogging toward the store. The last few days were weighing heavy on me. I was drained, and my energy was continuing to drop despite having a full stomach. If I didn't hurry this up and go to sleep, I might accidentally flash my fangs and shock poor old Tim. Or worse, shift into a bat and scare the man into an early grave.

The bell rang above my head as I pushed the heavy door open.

"Be right there!" an unfamiliar voice called out from the rear of the store.

A moment later, a woman who I guessed to be around Tim's age stepped out from between two towering stacks of boxes. Her gray hair flew around her face, and her long skirt trailed the floor. For a moment, I thought maybe I'd summoned a ghost.

"Sorry about the holdup." She used a handkerchief to wipe her face. "I had to step into the backroom to send out a few emails. How can I help you?"

My mood deflated. As sweet as this lady seemed to be, I didn't know how to break it to her that she couldn't help me. I searched the store for an item to buy so I didn't come off like a complete waste of time. My fingers locked around the first thing I could reach, and I held it up.

"Just the mustard, then?"

I looked at my hand and the large bottle of mustard in it. *Seriously, that's what I picked?* Cringing, I placed the bottle on the counter as the woman slid around the side to ring me up. "I ran out."

"Sure thing, honey," the woman said. "Will that be all?"

"Actually, I was looking for Tim Burr. Is he in today?"

The woman's white brows rose a little, and she narrowed her pale eyes on me through the acrylic shield between us. "What do you need with my Timmy?"

Ah. This must be his wife, then.

I hadn't noticed a ring the last time I was here, but not every man wore one. My dad had stopped sporting his the first time he transformed and lost the stupidly expensive ring down a manhole. Mom didn't let him live it down for months. Even threatened to glue the next one to his finger. But it wasn't long before they agreed it made more sense for him to quit wearing one since he had a habit of shifting and losing things at the worst possible time.

While I didn't think Tim was in quite the same situation as my vampire parents, there were plenty of reasons for him not to have a wedding band on.

I cleared my throat and slid a ten across the counter. "Oh, I met him the other day. Didn't realize he was married. It's a pleasure to meet you."

"You too, hun," the woman said. "I'm Calli, by the way. Maybe I can help in my husband's place."

"Lia," I offered. "And possibly. I was a friend of Polly Ester from down the street."

Calli's eyes watered, and she pressed a hand on her chest. "Poor woman. I'm sorry for your loss."

If guilt had a face, it would be mine. I was trying to do the right thing and find out what happened to Polly and Justin, but it still didn't feel right to lie to her. I uncurled my back and stood a little taller.

"Thank you. We weren't very close, but what happened was terrible." My eyebrows drew together. "Anyhow, this might sound strange. I'm curious if you and your husband own any property other than this store?"

"Not anymore."

"I'm sorry?"

Behind the glass, Calli's features darkened. For the first time since she'd appeared, the woman didn't have a smile on her face. In fact, she looked pretty angry.

"When Tim and I bought this place, we planned to expand. His side of the family was big into off-shore sales, and Tim had his eyes on getting into the family business." She looked out the dusty window, her lips down-turned. "I was fine with our little store here, but my Timmy, he had bigger plans. Convinced me to take over the lease on some rotten old warehouse that's been in his family for ages and promised we would turn it into an expansion of the store."

She shrugged.

"For a while, I was on board. I didn't care much for the area, but Tim promised it would turn around," she explained. "'The times are changing,' he'd say. 'People want big department stores and organic groceries.' That warehouse was his plan for our retirement."

"It's an impressive plan," I said, offering a smile.

Calli slammed a hand on the counter, startling me. "It's a fool's plan, is what it was. The land tax was too much as it is, and then when we got robbed, well, we simply couldn't afford the added expense."

"So you sold the warehouse?"

"Ha!" Calli guffawed. "I wish we sold right there and then. But no. Tim decided we needed to push on. 'It's the perfect place, Calli,' he said. 'Even has a panic room; we know we'll be safe there.' I'm still not sure who or what he hoped to save us from. After all, the robbers weren't targeting us specifically. They just saw the store as a quick cash grab."

The woman's scowl told me the two had plenty of arguments over the warehouse, and I wondered if I'd opened a can of worms that could detonate their marriage. As though sensing my discomfort, she rubbed her jaw and flashed a warm smile, the same one she'd given me when I'd first seen her.

"The thing about marriage is that the only way to make it work is someone usually has to back down. Sometimes it's you, sometimes it's your partner, but there's no room for two goats on a narrow, one-way bridge," she said. "They don't tell you that when you're young, huh?"

I chuckled under my breath. "Not exactly. I take it you still own the warehouse?"

"Heck, no!" Calli slapped her hand down on the counter. "Not sure if you heard, but most of the other businesses that got taken also had to close shop and ended up selling their land shortly after. These monsters aren't out there targeting the big corporations. No, they're coming after those of us having trouble keeping doors open as it is."

She sighed, her head shaking. "Tim couldn't see it, but I sure could. I told him unless he wanted to spend our retirement living on the street, he'd smarten up and help me sell the place."

"Did he?"

"Why, of course, honey!" Calli grinned and pointed to her forehead. "I'm the goat with the bigger horns in this family."

Laughing again, I leaned in closer to the woman. "Do you happen to remember who bought it?"

"Couldn't tell you even if I wanted to, dear." Calli shook her head. "It was an anonymous buyer. Got the place for dirt cheap, too, but at that point, I was glad to be rid of the burden. Why all the interest in it?"

"No specific reason," I said quickly. "Polly mentioned it in passing, and it stuck with me."

Holding up the mustard, I waved it again like a complete idiot and said, "Thanks for the condiment."

Leaving Calli looking confused, I bolted out the door before I said anything else embarrassing and took off down the street. What a colossal waste of time this had been. I made a mental note to tell Skeeter that the lead was a dead end and speed-walked down the street.

My eyelids were droopy, and my legs dragged as I made my way to my car. The conversation with Calli led nowhere, though if I was being honest, I wasn't sure what I thought I'd find out.

It wasn't as though I'd even considered Tim Burr as a suspect. The man was sweet as pie and had no reason to hurt Polly. As far as I knew, he'd never even met Justin, so there was no connection between the two murders.

Still, the warehouse had seemed like a promising lead, and the disappointment I nurtured over hitting a dead end was palpable. Refusing to postpone a much-needed nap any longer, I crawled into the car and made my way home, where I barely made it to bed before I passed out.

Sometimes, all a vamp needed was a pillow and six hours of shuteye.

CHAPTER EIGHTEEN

S leep was an evasive son of a biscuit eater, slipping through my grasp like sand through my fingers. No matter how hard I tried, I couldn't seem to find a good day's rest. Each time I drifted off, my thoughts yanked me back to consciousness, rudely dragging me out of dreamland. The weight of the events of the last few weeks bore down on me heavily, a burden I couldn't seem to shake off.

The relentless hustle and bustle of the clinic over the past few months added to my restlessness. Its growing demands and my limited staff left me often feeling under-prepared and overwhelmed. My need to unravel the mysteries surrounding Polly and now Justin just added to my gloomy thoughts.

I rolled over in bed; I'd forgotten to turn on the fan, and

the sheets were tangled around my damp legs like seaweed, and a fine sheen of sweat coated my skin. After a few more failed attempts to sleep, I tossed the thin blanket off me and onto the floor and got up. Sliding the blinds open, I hissed when the sun hit my eyes, blinding me temporarily. Shielding them with my hand, I made my way to the kitchen for a blood box and an ice pack to ease the headache pounding my skull.

As I padded down the hallway, what Justin's sister had said slowly came back to me. Exactly how much money trouble had my tech been in before he died?

The question I really wanted to ask but didn't even dare to speak out loud was causing my stomach to feel like I'd swallowed several pounds of lead. Was it a deep enough debt to make it worth the risk of killing Polly if he'd found out she was behind the robberies?

I pushed the thought away, not wanting to picture my vet tech as a heartless killer. Opening the fridge, I pulled out a much-needed refreshment and was halfway through draining the blood box when there was a sharp knock on my front door.

Pulse skyrocketing, I wiped my mouth and tossed the rest of the box in the trash, annoyed I didn't get to finish.

"Coming!" I yelled as a second knock echoed through my house.

Who was here? I didn't like admitting it, but in all the time I'd lived in Bluejay Falls, I hadn't made many friends. Sure, there was Skeeter, who I supposed was as close to a friend as I could get. And Ashley at The Roastery could probably be counted as a friend as well, but for the most part, I was a loner.

Most vampires ran in groups called covens, but not me. I enjoyed being self-reliant and not depending on other people. Although, even I could admit, a solitary lifestyle got lonely at times.

When I opened the door, I was surprised to find a friendly face on the other side.

"Morning," Bree chirped, holding out a paper bag.

Taking the bag, I peered inside.

Seeing my confusion, the pixie explained, "I brought lunch. Well, lunch for me and a blood box for you. It's under the sandwich."

Wait, what? Bree and I never saw each other outside the clinic except for that one awkward time I bumped into her at the bar. Literally. I'd flown into that poor girl like I was aiming to magic myself straight through her. Drinks had flown everywhere, and I would've been squashed beneath a troll's heavy boot if she hadn't scooped me off the floor and cradled me in her arms as though I were one of our patients.

After that, I vowed to never hang out in the same area as my employees ever again. Except one was now standing with a foot in my house and a bag of food in her hands. What was going on?

Perhaps I was being *Punk'd*? "I don't remember making plans..."

"We didn't, and I know we don't really do this," Bree said, sensing my confusion.

And yet...

When she kept staring up at me without showing any hints of leaving, I could feel my resolve beginning to crumble.

Bree grinned, "You have to admit, it's kinda funny that I'm waiting for a vampire to give me permission to enter her house. Isn't it supposed to be the other way around?"

Unable to help myself, I laughed and stepped aside to allow her entry. Bree skipped across the threshold with a familiarity I didn't expect, as though this wasn't her first time in my home when we both knew that wasn't the case. Watching her with curiosity, I couldn't help but notice the subtle gleam of approval that danced in her eyes as they swept over my humble house.

"Cute place," she said, her words carrying a sincere warmth that matched the smile stretching on her face.

The pixie deposited the bag she carried onto the kitchen island, emptying its contents and arranging them in a neat line on the countertop. Pulling out a chair, she sat down and grabbed the sandwich. Without waiting for me to join her, she took a bite and moaned in satisfaction.

Turning toward me, Bree wiped a line of mustard from her chin and placed the sandwich back on the counter. "We need to talk about what happened to Justin."

Those words hit me like holy water to the face... although, technically, holy water didn't bother vampires any more than garlic did.

My clammy fingers burrowed into the wood paneling of the doorway as I clung to it for dear life. I wasn't ready to discuss Justin. More than that, I didn't want to do it with my employee, who was probably scarred for life now. Couldn't I just pay for her to go to therapy with a professional? Sharing feelings wasn't really a trait vampires were known for possessing.

My throat bobbed as I swallowed. Hard. "What about him?"

"Give me a break, boss," Bree said. "The guy was straight up murdered in our alleyway a few feet from where we work. There is a lot about him we need to discuss. And don't tell me you're buying the whole random act thing the cops are spewing. Not after one of our patients also ended up dead under equally mysterious circumstances."

She bit into her sandwich, chewed, and then swallowed. "Especially since the two didn't get along."

I had no clue Bree felt this way or that she was coming to the same conclusions as I was. My plan to try and keep Bree away from the negativity of the murders had failed spectacularly, and she'd come up with theories of her own. And she'd decided to come here of all places to discuss it. With me. Why?

My gaze landed on the blood box she'd brought and the half-eaten sandwich across from it. Were we becoming... *friends*?

Clearing my throat, I watched the pixie closely, wanting to gauge her honest reaction. "If I share information with you I think is important, will you promise not to go to the police with it? At least not right away?"

"Heck, yes!" The pixie clapped her hands. "What did you find out? I know you've been snooping."

"How did you know?" I asked.

Bree pointed to her head and wiggled her eyebrows. "Pixie, remember? Reading people is sorta my thing. That, and I overheard you talking to Skeeter."

Laughing under my breath, I skirted around the island and rested my elbows on the table. The counter felt cool against my skin, and, for the first time in hours, a sense of calmness settled over me. The sweat-soaking my clothes was starting to dry, and I could feel the headache that thrummed between my temples easing. It would be nice to have someone to talk about all this.

I sucked in a breath between my clenched teeth and met the pixie's eyes. Then I told her what I'd uncovered so far. While spilling my guts, I made sure to keep some things to myself because I didn't want Bree getting in trouble for interfering with the investigation if it ever came to that. Ignorance was bliss sometimes, or so I'd heard. By the time I was done, I was out of breath, and Bree was in the loop. Mostly.

Bree remained quiet, her luminous eyes batting like a baby deer in a children's movie. Finally, she propped her elbows on the table and rested her chin against her palms. "His sister really said he had a gambling addiction?"

"That's what you got from all of that?"

The pixie smirked. "No, but that part stood out. I can see

why you'd think Justin might kill Polly for cash if he thought she was behind the robberies." She sighed. "For the record, I don't know if I buy that. But it sure fits as a motive, doesn't it?"

I nodded. "And there's no solid evidence Polly was even responsible for those."

"Right," Bree agreed. "She could have been killed because she figured out who it was."

Sticking the straw in the crimson box, I took a long sip before adding, "Or she was in on it and had a partner who wanted her out of the picture. I don't think it's too outrageous to think criminals might double-cross each other."

The pixie stared off into the distance, her eyes glassy and unfocused. Her breathing grew shallow, and I had to check if her chest was moving at all to make sure she was still alive. Whatever was on Bree's mind, it had her in a trance.

A second later, her pupils refocused, and she snapped her head to face me, a sparkle in her eyes. "Oh! Don't forget the way Polly was killed."

My body stilled. "The stethoscope. Of course."

This entire time, I'd been running around looking for clues to get to the bottom of what happened, and I'd completely forgotten about the stethoscope. It was the one thing that painted a definitive red X on Justin's back as the killer. I wondered if the police had come to the same conclusion and made a mental note to see what I could get out of Ryder later.

Perhaps I could pay the detective a visit and work out a

deal? Perhaps if I offered up what I had on the case, he might go easy on me.

A part of me really wanted to believe that. But another part of me, the one that was realistic and had seen too many murder documentaries, knew I was in way too deep now. Not only had I possibly withheld critical information from the cops, but I'd also dragged two innocent bystanders into this mess.

On second thought, maybe this wasn't the time to contact Ryder. Not yet. I needed more solid information to bring to him first. Something that would make all the laws I'd possibly broken seem unimportant in the grand scheme of things.

Like figuring out who the killer was, for example.

Or the robbers' identities.

I was sure that if I gave Ryder a lead that big, he'd give me a slap on the wrist and not arrest me. And hopefully, he'd even look the other way about Bree and Skeeter being involved.

Focusing my attention back on Bree, I bit the inside of my cheek and asked, "How hard do you think it would be to find out if Justin's sister was right about his money problems?"

"Hard," the pixie replied, deflating my hopes, then her eyebrows wiggled mischievously.

I suppressed a smile, realizing Bree had a sneaky little plan in mind.

Leaning in close, the pixie tucked a brightly colored

strand of hair behind her ear and whispered, "Unless you happened to have his social security number."

Well, would you look at that? As Justin's employer, it just so happened I had the exact thing she was looking for.

The morning rushed by as we scoured the depths of the internet, determined to uncover something that would help our investigation. Despite hitting a number of dead ends, we managed to track down one solid lead. Justin's bank name. Bree used her knowledge from months of working alongside him to guess his password.

With a stroke of ingenuity, Bree deciphered the secret combination—Justin's birthday in reverse, followed by an exclamation mark. Not the most secure choice, but I doubted Justin counted on anyone breaking into his online banking.

After having to guess the answers to several security questions, we were in.

One look at Justin's transactions for the last few months confirmed it. He was broke.

"Wow," Bree breathed out. "He spent a lot of time at the casino two towns over."

"Seems his sister wasn't lying," I confirmed.

We looked at the statements for the past few months, then went as far back as last year, but Justin's financial records held a very telling story.

As Bess had mentioned, he'd inherited quite a bit when their parents died. What she forgot to disclose was that Justin also got a large sum of life insurance from his parents' death that he blew through almost immediately. That left him with only his salary from the clinic to sustain him, and he didn't appear to be doing a stellar job of keeping that balanced well. All of Justin's expenses were frivolous. From bills at pricey restaurants for his dates to more trips to casinos—Justin was living well beyond his means.

From what I could see, he was on a fast track to complete bankruptcy.

"If I was Justin, and I saw a way to get out from under all this debt, I'd jump on it," Bree said, frowning.

Sadly, I had to agree. While I still had my reservations about Justin committing murder, the evidence was becoming harder to ignore. My tech had a life I knew nothing about, one that may have taken him on a dark path. Between confirming what Bess had said, the stethoscope, and the gum I'd found in Polly's backyard, the signs pointing to Justin might as well have been flashing with neon lights.

Justin Case killed Polly. Or, at the very least, he'd had a connection to her and her death. Either way, it did not look good for him.

Outside, the sun had risen high in the sky, and I checked the time, surprised to find we'd been at this for hours. We spent another half hour at the island while Bree finished the cheesecake she'd brought, and I gulped down another Crimson Quench. Despite my rules for not mixing work with pleasure, I'd had fun that morning, and it was so much better to have someone to use as a sounding board for my wild ideas and theories.

As I shut the door behind Bree, my shoulders drooped in relief. I was close to a big discovery here. I could feel it in my fangs. Soon, I was going to have enough to bring to Ryder. I looked at the couch in the living room, hearing it call my name.

Sleep first. Stress later.

CHAPTER NINETEEN

Wings flapped over my head as Byrd crash-landed in a pile of clothes in my closet. Coming in hot, Elvis screeched and dove in pursuit of the bat. Loud chittering and squawks filled the bedroom.

I rolled over in bed and pressed a pillow to my ear, hoping to drown out the racket, but it was no use. The winged duo was far too loud.

They had been at it for the last twenty minutes, and as much as I wanted to stay in bed and relax, having a bat and parrot go at it had to be the most obnoxious alarm clock on earth. Seriously, I could record the sound and make an app of it. It would sell like hotcakes.

"Can't wake up in the mornings? Try the Barrot alarm!"

"Losing your hearing? Try the Barrot alarm!"

"Accidentally ingested bear sedatives? Try the Barrot alarm!"

You get the drift.

I wiggled my legs to free them and swung them over the bed, groggily dragging myself up. My hair was a matted mess, and I left the rascals to battle it out in the closet while I went to the bathroom to clean up.

As much as I hated to admit it, they were pretty cute together. It was nice to see Byrd do something other than nap and snack, and Elvis was really coming into his own. There were even moments when I could tell he was having fun despite still grieving for his beloved owner.

People often forget how much our pets rely on us. With Polly gone and his life turned upside down, Elvis didn't know how to behave, and it was heartwarming to see him showing a fraction of his feisty self—even if it did take playing tag with a lazy bat to do it.

I raked wet fingers through my curls, the strands clinging together with residual moisture as I attempted to tame them back into place. Gathering the unruly mane into a messy bun atop my head, I pulled out a few stray tendrils to make it look like I'd been aiming for a cool, grunge look.

After brushing my teeth, I made a beeline for the kitchen, my stomach growling like a rabid werewolf. The refrigerator door swung open with a soft creak, and my gaze fell on the familiar boxes of Crimson Quench. The tangy scent teased my nostrils as I reached for the chilled box, sending anticipation coursing through me at the promise of food.

As I took a long, refreshing swig, my attention was drawn to the island countertop where my phone lay, its screen lighting up momentarily before dimming into darkness once more. A knot formed in my stomach. With a final gulp, I downed the rest of the Crimson Quench and reached for the phone.

The display revealed I'd missed several calls. Drawing a steadying breath, I punched in the all-too-familiar number. My heart pounded in my chest as I waited for the call to connect.

It rang once, barely, before someone picked up.

"Marty! She's alive! You can call off the bat patrol!"

"Hi, Mom. I saw you called." I rolled my eyes at my parents' dramatics and added, "Eleven times."

"Darling, you are our only daughter. We are allowed to worry. So, how are things? How's the clinic?"

And it begins...

I knew my mother well enough to know what she really wanted to know was if I'd met anyone yet. My love life had become the main topic of conversation since I turned thirty and had yet to settle down with—Mom's words, not mine— a down-to-earth vamp who would worship the ground I walked on and could rip off a man's head simply for looking at me. Bonus points if said vamp also liked animals, but at this point, Mom would settle for anyone with half a fang.

She'd brought it up so many times it had become a staple at family gatherings. Not only that, but she'd gotten the extended family on board, and now I had to dodge great-aunts and uncles three times removed at every family reunion.

So when Mom asked about the clinic, I immediately knew it was code for something else. Pretending to be clueless, I walked to the couch and sat down, throwing my feet up on the coffee table.

"The clinic is great." I winced. "Except my vet tech sort of… died."

"No! Not the pixie!" My mom exclaimed. "She was adorable."

"No, the human. Justin."

Mom breathed out a sigh of relief. "Oh, good. Well, not good. I just really didn't want it to be that sweet girl. What happened?"

As I opened my mouth to explain, Elvis shot through the room with Byrd on his heels. They circled around me, the wind from their wings causing my hair to fly around my face. I waved my free arm over my head to keep the beasts at bay.

"The police don't know yet, or at least they haven't told me anything."

"The police?" Mom's voice spiked a few octaves. "Why are the police involved? Please tell me it's not what I think it is."

I bit my lower lip. "It's nothing for you to worry over, Mom."

"Nothing to—Ophelia Pane. How many times do I have to tell you I will worry until I'm dead? Which is hopefully many years from now unless you send me to an early grave

194

from stress. You know you would be a lot safer working all hours of the night if you had a—"

"Don't say it," I interrupted.

Pretending she didn't hear me, Mom barreled ahead. "A strong vampire boyfriend to watch over you. Your father and I do not like knowing you are out there all on your own. Why don't you consider what we suggested?"

I wasn't sure how to decline their offer to move in with them politely. My mouth opened, but I closed it again as Elvis zoomed by.

"A star and its center! A star and its center!" he screamed at the top of his lungs.

"What was that?" Mom asked.

"A parrot I'm babysitting." I rubbed my tired eyes, leaving out the part about his owner dying because my mom didn't need anything else to stress over. "It's a bit of a zoo here right now."

"Darling, it is always..." She paused. "Hang on a sec. Marty! Put that blood box down if you know what's good for you! That's your fourth one in two hours, and you know how you get when you're overfed!" She sighed. "Sorry, what did you say?"

Laughing, I stretched out on the couch, watching Elvis and Byrd continue their chase. "Never mind."

"All right, well, promise you will think about what we said," she begged. "Take a look at the map I sent of that adorable neighborhood near us. It would be a great spot for a clinic."

After promising her I'd check out the area and assuring

her I'd check in the next day, I ended the call and sank back into the comfort of my pillow.

Elvis circled above me, his colorful feathers catching the light. It was mesmerizing, and with each pass, he seemed to carry away a bit more of the haze that clouded my mind.

As the fog dissipated, my eyes snapped wide open. I found myself sitting bolt upright, a sudden clarity seizing my thoughts like a vice. A map. It hadn't triggered anything when my mother mentioned it, but now, a crucial piece of a puzzle seemed to click into place.

I rushed to the bedroom and dug into an old box in my closet with a bunch of junk I had to sort through since the move. After searching through the mess, I pulled out an old map of the state and ran back into the living room. Using the only free wall across from the television, I taped the map up and ripped off the cap of a marker I found in the junk drawer.

Working from memory, I made a dot for every robbery noted in Polly's book that I could remember. When my memory failed me, I referenced the translation of the short-hand code that Skeeter provided so I could add the rest. Then, I connected the dots.

Stepping back, my jaw hitting the ground. "Elvis, you brilliant son of a bird!"

The pattern created by the robbery locations formed a perfect star on the map. Pressing my finger to the paper, I traced down and over, forming another connection until I hit the exact center of the star shape.

Behind me, the parrot squawked, and Byrd chittered in response, but I was barely paying attention. My focus was only on the big X I'd marked on the map.

"Well, marinate me in garlic and stake me through the heart!"

CHAPTER TWENTY

O f all the ways to catch a break, a clue from a chatty parrot was not how I'd imagined it would go down. I'd never watched a detective show where the case was blown wide open by a loud-mouthed bird. There was a decent chance I was grasping at straws, and this was not the earth-shattering discovery I had thought it was.

So why, then, was I standing in my living room, staring at a map of crimes that had Polly's oddball neighbor Dusty's house smack dab in the center?

Perhaps Elvis wasn't spewing nonsense after all. Was there a chance the parrot had been trying to point me in the right direction this entire time? It was a stretch, and yet I couldn't let it go.

Grinding my teeth, I walked backward until my legs hit the couch. Eyes trained on the big X I'd drawn, I reached for my purse and dug around for my cell phone and the card Ryder had left me. It was time to do what I should have done long ago and come clean with the detective.

I dreaded hearing his voice, but it'd be foolish not to tell him what I'd found out. Especially since there might actually be a valid reason for them to investigate someone further.

My gaze flicked to Elvis perched on a barstool. A semi-valid reason, at least.

Nerves spiking, I swallowed the lump in my throat and waited as Ryder's line rang several times. My nails tapped out a fast rhythm on the arm of the couch, and the sound earned me an annoyed hiss from Byrd, who was hiding in the depths of the kitchen. After a few more rings, I was sent through to voicemail. Great.

I waited for the beep, sucked in a breath, and belted out my message in a single run-on sentence. "Hi, Ryder—or Detective Ryder, I guess—you said to call you if I have any information, and I do, sort of, maybe. I don't know if it makes sense, but I'll let you be the judge of that, it's Lia Pane, the vet, by the way, call me back when you have a chance."

I hung up and threw the phone on the couch like it was a bomb about to explode. From the corner of my eye, I caught Elvis staring at me, his head cocked all the way to one side.

"What? Don't judge me! I got nervous."

"A star and its center," Elvis answered, ruffling his feathers.

I sighed, glancing back at the map. "I know, buddy, I know."

Scanning the locations, I noted the robberies and scratched my chin. "Notice how all of them were on the outskirts of town where the police jurisdiction changes? That explains why it's been so hard to catch these guys. Except the Grab 'n Go. That one is in the middle of all the action. I wonder why."

When Elvis didn't answer, I walked back to the wall and put my finger on Dusty's house. It was strange that the parrot continued to point out the center of the pattern and even stranger that it pointed directly to the woman who'd been very vocal about her dislike of Polly.

Was there a chance Dusty wasn't as innocent as she made herself out to be? I knew something hadn't felt right when I was in her house. What if it was because, deep down, I knew she was up to no good?

When it came to animals, I had almost a sixth sense about what they needed or were about to do. Maybe I had the same sense for people...

It wouldn't be the first time a paranormal had a special ability that fell outside their species' norms.

I laughed at myself. Who was I kidding? I couldn't even transform without getting a headache. What were the chances I had somehow developed a new ability this late in life? Less than zero.

Grabbing my phone, I tapped the screen. Still no callback from Ryder. My eyes landed on the parrot, who continued to watch me with a serious expression. Unable to stand around doing nothing, I rolled my shoulders and typed another number into my phone. "Skeeter?" I asked when the troll picked up. "Think you can track someone down for me?"

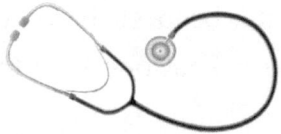

PROMENADE PARK, nestled in the heart of our bustling town, was a picturesque oasis frequented by both locals and tourists alike. Enclosed by large iron gates and towering oak trees that reached for the sky, the park possessed an enchanting ambiance.

As I strolled along the winding cobblestone pathway that ran through the park, I found myself entranced by my surroundings. The landscape, adorned with vibrant flora, drew the eye and lightened the heart. Around every corner, there was a new marvel to behold, like the pond that reflected the sky above while its surface gently rippled in the breeze or the labyrinth created with hedges that added a sense of mystery to the perfectly manicured garden. If you weren't careful, you could easily get lost in its beauty and lose track of time.

Despite the park being less crowded today, its beauty remained the same, perhaps even heightened by the companionable silence. The distant sounds of the town faded into the background, allowing the sounds of nature to take center stage.

Here, time seemed to slow down, allowing visitors to take a break from the quick pace of everyday life. It was truly magical.

Following Skeeter's directions, I cut across a narrow bridge and emerged on the edge of a clearing. Shielding my eyes from the sun, I scanned the grass, being careful not to wipe off the thick layer of sunscreen I'd applied just before leaving the house.

Just as Skeeter had predicted, Dusty was smack dab in the action of a yoga class. Long mats in a variety of colors were spread out on the grass in a semi-circle around their teacher. There was a good mix of people in the class, and I was shocked when I saw a woman older than my mother do a handstand. I cringed, thinking of my lack of coordination. *Maybe I should consider taking a yoga class sometime.*

A younger man rolled himself into a tiny pretzel, and I felt every muscle in my body protest. On second thought, perhaps yoga wasn't for me.

I parked myself on an iron bench facing the group, my back pressing against a cool bronze plate, showing that the bench was dedicated to some guy who died decades ago. While I waited for the class to finish, I tried not to make eye contact with Dusty and instead studied the rest of the benches scattered around me. There a similar bronze plate on each one, with another inscription featuring another unknown name. It felt odd to sit amid all the dedications, almost like I was in a graveyard, lounging on a tombstone.

Shifting my weight, I swallowed the discomfort and

pretended to scroll on my phone, keeping one eye on the yoga class. On the outskirts of the yoga mats, Dusty raised a wobbly leg in the air and pressed her forehead to the mat. The half-a-gazillion beads she wore dangled from her neck, and she wiggled a bit, trying to get them out from beneath her. Instead, a spluttering Dusty lost her balance, which sent her tumbling to the ground with a thud.

I stifled a laugh.

According to Skeeter, the class Dusty took every week ended in ten minutes, but I wondered if she'd last until the end, considering her current starfish pose on the mat. Pure relief washed over her face when the teacher announced a closing pose. Clearly, she was more than ready for this thing to be over.

As the students rolled up their mats, I timed my entrance to the second. Taking out my phone, I put it up to my face and started to walk in Dusty's direction, aiming my body so that I would barrel straight into her.

Keeping my eyes locked on the screen, I picked up speed as the distance between us closed. As planned, our bodies collided. Summoning my non-existent acting skills, I stumbled backward, feigning surprise.

"I'm so sorry," I yelped, looking up from my phone for the first time. "I wasn't paying attention— Oh! Dusty! What a surprise!"

Dusty looked at me with bulging eyes. "Hello again." She searched her mind for my name but was unsuccessful. "What are you doing here?"

"I usually come here to think," I lied. "I didn't realize

they do yoga here. Do you like it? I've been thinking about trying a class."

My inquiry seemed to excite Dusty, and I watched as her face lit up with the opportunity to sell me on the idea. I should have known this would be the best way to lure her into a conversation; she struck me as someone who loved to hear herself talk.

Dusty switched her mat from one shoulder to the other. "You should definitely join," she said eagerly. "It is an eye-opening experience. And you'd be surprised how limber you can be. I shock myself every week."

Images of her falling over flashed in my mind, and I struggled to keep a straight face.

"I will keep that in mind," I told Dusty. "But now that I ran into you, any chance you could help me out?"

Glancing at her watch, she took a step back, a clear sign she was not planning on chatting for long.

I raised my arms, saying, "It will only take a minute, I promise."

"Well, I suppose that's fine," she said. "What can I do for you?"

"I was wondering if you noticed any strange activity in your neighborhood? People who don't live there hanging about or anything else that struck you as odd."

Her eyes narrowed. "Why do you ask? Is something else happening on my street? I haven't been told a thing, and if there is cause for alarm, all the residents should have been made aware."

Arms still up in surrender, I plastered on my most

welcoming smile, all teeth showing. Relaxing my shoulders, I tried to look as comfortable and natural as I could, not wanting to put Dusty even more on edge.

"Nothing so scary," I laughed, trying to disarm her. "I've been watching too much of the news, I'm afraid. These robberies happening all over the state have me tied up in knots. I notice they seem to be getting closer and closer to our little town. One happened right on your street!"

"Finally!" Dusty exclaimed. "Someone else who thinks it's weird!"

I tried to hide my interest, cocking my head to the side. "You noticed the strangeness too?"

"Well, of course!" she exclaimed. "I simply don't understand how the police haven't caught up to these horrible people yet. But to answer your question, no, nothing odd in our area that I can recall. Come to think of it, Polly was also very interested in the robberies."

I quirked a brow. "Oh?"

"Very," Dusty enunciated. "Her and Tristan got into quite the heated argument over the topic a few weeks back."

My ears perked up at that juicy tidbit. "Your son?"

Dusty's lips tightened into a thin line, and she nodded.

"Do you recall what they argued over?"

"Beats me," she said with a careless shrug. "But I remember Tristan stomping in the house red as a ripe tomato. He said Polly needed to learn to mind her own business. I guess whatever that loose-lipped gossip said to him hit a nerve. I'd never seen my boy so upset."

Interesting.

I rolled my tongue over my front teeth and leaned in closer. "Has your son ever said anything about the Grab 'n Go robbery? Maybe that's what they talked about."

"Not really," Dusty said, causing my hope to deflate until she added, "But he hasn't been on the best terms with the Burrs since they fired him."

Chest suddenly tight, I tried to take a deep breath and failed. My lips puckered, and I gave a low whistle between my teeth. "Tristan worked at the Grab 'n Go?"

"Sure did," Dusty replied. "My sweet boy is always helping people. Went so far as to offer Tim to fix up that junkyard of a warehouse his family owned. But then they fired him out of nowhere, using a made-up story about making ends meet. Tristan was devastated."

She met my gaze. "I haven't stepped foot in that nasty little store since. The nerve of some people!"

My head spun. The Burrs hadn't mentioned employing Tristan, but then again, why would they? What stuck out to me most was Tristan's offer to fix up the warehouse. Why would he care about some old, empty commercial graveyard in the middle of nowhere? And why be so upset over a part-time job at a convenience store?

Most importantly, what was the disagreement he and Polly had over the robberies?

I was about to ask Dusty more questions when my phone buzzed, stopping me in my tracks. Glancing down, I felt my stomach drop to my toes.

"Everything all right?" Dusty asked, craning her neck to peer at my screen.

My mouth had gone dry, and I didn't think I could have answered if I tried. I couldn't do anything but stare at the alert from the security system telling me the back door alarm had been tripped.

Someone had broken into the Sunny Days Clinic.

CHAPTER TWENTY-ONE

When people read fantasy books, especially the ones that had been around long enough to be considered lore, they assumed vampires were indestructible. That most of us could be thrown off a roof and *poof!* —we were saved by our bat wings. While sure, the wings were cool, and they could save you a pinch, that wasn't the whole story.

What the stories always forgot to mention, and what I was figuring out pretty dang quickly as I approached the ajar back door of the clinic, was that fanged blood-sucker or not, some of us were scared of their own shadow if the conditions were right.

My knees were nearly banging against each other as I reached for the handle. At the last second, I yanked my fingers away as though the metal was made of molten lava.

Yep. I was a freaking scaredy-bat.

My stomach churned as the weight of what I might find on the other side of the door finally hit me. What was I thinking rushing into this on my own? There was every chance whoever broke into the clinic was still there, possibly armed.

I blew out a humorless chuckle under my breath. *Who breaks into a veterinary clinic with a gun?*

Not wanting to go forward but not ready to retreat, I glanced behind me at the empty alley, my eyes avoiding the dumpster where Justin's body had been found.

Taking in several deep breaths, I tried to calm my frayed nerves with a dose of logic. Realistically, this was nothing more than a malfunction with the alarm, or maybe Bree had forgotten her coat and tripped it accidentally. It wouldn't be the first time. At least, that was what I told myself as I bit down on the inside of my cheek and pulled the handle.

The door swung open fast, the force of the adrenaline running through my body, giving it wings. I teetered back, barely avoiding getting smacked in the forehead by the thick metal by mere centimeters. Poking my nose through the opening, I tried to see if anyone was inside without going inside myself, but I couldn't make anything out.

A low shuffle sounded in the distance, and I gulped. "Nope. This is so not happening today."

I turned around and darted back down the alley. Leaning against the clinic wall, I pulled out my phone.

The phone rang three times before a gruff voice answered. "Detective Wolff."

"Ryder!" I yelled, then collected myself and added,

"Sorry. Detective. I need you to send someone down to the clinic. I think it was broken into, and I don't know if they're still inside."

A throat cleared on the line. "Who is this?"

"Oh. Right. It's Lia. Lia Pane."

"Miss Pane, are you at the clinic right now?"

I winced. "Yes. I'm in the alley out back."

"All right. Stay there and wait for me. I'll be there shortly." There was a rustle, then he spoke again. "And Miss Pane?"

"Yes, Detective?"

"Don't go inside."

The line went dead, and I rested my head back against the wall. In my chest, my heart was pounding, and my pulse was thrumming so fast I could feel the blood rushing through my veins.

Stay put. I could totally do that. That was the smart move, and I could totally wait for the detective to get here, the guy with the gun.

But what if Bree was inside? Worse, what if something had happened to her, and she was hurt?

My eyes darted to the dumpster, and a shiver rolled up my spine. I'd already lost one vet tech, and I couldn't in good conscience stand around and do nothing if there was even a chance someone I cared about needed help.

Then again, what if I was right the first time, and whoever had tripped the alarm was in the clinic waiting for me to come in?

The 'what ifs' were exhausting. I knew without a doubt

that staying outside would mean driving myself insane until Ryder finally made an appearance. I didn't even know when he would show up. For all I knew, he had to make a few stops before he came for a simple security alarm call.

By then, it could be too late.

Taking excruciatingly slow steps, I inched closer to the open door. My fangs popped out with a hiss, and I ran my tongue over them, feeling slightly better about my odds. Worst-case scenario, I scared the life out of whoever was inside. I could always claim they were Halloween props.

Slinking through the opening, I waited for my eyes to adjust to the low light and walked deeper into the dark clinic.

Here's hoping it's only Bree, flustered because she couldn't find something she'd forgotten.

I knew the layout of the place like the back of my hand, so it took no time to clear the kitchenette and slide further down the hallway. A gust of wind blew the door shut behind me, and I jumped, stifling a yelp as my back crashed into the wall.

Tightening my jaw, I half crawled, half walked the rest of the way, checking each crevice and corner. When I got to the first examination room, I reached for the handle and then paused.

One... two... three...

My breath hitched as I twisted the handle, turning it slowly so as not to make a sound, and used the tip of my index finger to push it open. Creeping inside, I found it was empty.

Proceeding through the dark clinic like a mouse looking for cheese, I checked two more rooms with the same result. So far, it appeared there was no need to panic, and I felt a pang of guilt for calling Ryder. If the detective didn't already think I was off my rocker, this complete waste of his time was sure to convince him.

I started for the waiting room when a loud clatter nearly burst my eardrums. There was no doubt about it. Someone was definitely inside the clinic with me. Skin crawling, I turned on my heels, rushing to get the heck out of dodge.

My face smashed into a hard object, and my neck cracked as I was catapulted back down the hallway. Fangs dug into my lip, drawing blood. A sharp headache ricocheted between my temples as I tried to shake off my confusion.

Eyes widening at the dark silhouette towering over me, I scrambled backward on my butt, trying to get away.

"Lia?"

I blinked. "Ryder?"

A large hand reached toward me, grabbed my hand and pulled me to my feet. His gaze rolled over me, stopping on my lips. "You're bleeding."

I pressed a finger to the drops of blood from where my fangs had punctured the skin. Closing my lips, I hurriedly retracted them before Ryder could spot them and quickly licked away the blood.

"Bit down too hard," I blushed. "You startled me."

"I thought I told you to stay put."

"Funny story," I said with an embarrassed chuckle. "I

was doing just that, but then I realized Bree might be hurt and had to check things out. You got here quicker than I thought you would."

Light glinted off an object in Ryder's hand, and my eyes snapped to the gun he had drawn. His brow creased, and for the first time, I noticed the worry on his face. It never occurred to me that when the detective had arrived and found me missing, he likely thought my idiotic self was hurt.

Brushing back the knotted mess of hair from my face, I met his eyes. "I probably should've waited."

"I'd say so," Ryder agreed. "I thought you were hurt or worse. It doesn't seem like there's anyone here. If someone broke in, they left before we got here. But I want to look around a bit more."

He motioned for me to get behind him, and I skirted around his broad frame. Ryder walked intentionally as we made our way toward the waiting room. I noticed the gun was still out, though he put the safety back on, which made me breathe a little better.

Looking left and right, Ryder cleared the room, his shoulders relaxing. I peered out over them to see if I could spot whatever it was I'd heard earlier, but there was nothing in sight. The noise must have come from the street, and, in my flustered state, I'd mistaken it for a person.

The last few days had me on edge, and it was beginning to show.

Ryder made another pass through the clinic, and when he was satisfied that the coast was clear, he asked me to turn on the lights. I walked to the reception desk and flicked switches one by one until we were blinded by the bright overhead lights.

With the fluorescents on full blast, the clinic no longer felt like a haunted horror house, and in my mind, I began laughing at my original panic. It was nothing more than a malfunction of the alarm, and I'd blown things way out of proportion. Not to mention, I'd dragged the detective down here to protect me because I was a wimpy vamp. He had far better things to do than babysit an anxious veterinarian.

I watched Ryder continue to search the premises while my guilt clawed at me.

When he finally holstered his gun, I asked, "Do you want a coffee? I can put a pot on."

"Actually, that would be great." Ryder smiled. "I'm going back to the station after this, and it might be a long night."

Leaving him to sit in one of the waiting room chairs, I made my way to the kitchenette. As I walked, I sent a text off to Bree in case she'd received the same alarm text and told her not to worry. Above me, the overhead lights flickered, and I made a mental note to replace them before they burned out.

Maybe I'd go ahead and do that after Ryder left. I may as well be productive since I was already at the clinic. As I walked into our small kitchen, I made a beeline for the coffee machine. It came alive with a whir, the familiar sound of roasting coffee filling the tiny space.

I was about to reach for a blood box from the hidden

compartment in the fridge when I turned around and stopped stock still. The mug in my hand dropped to the ground, shattering on impact. My lips parted, and a scream escaped me before I could stop it.

Down the hallway, footsteps pounded closer as Ryder rushed to the kitchenette. When he skidded to a stop beside me, gun drawn, we both stared in shock.

There, painted in bright red, smeared letters on the wall, was a message.

I shivered, reading aloud, "Back off, or you're next."

"Is that blood?" Ryder asked.

"No," I answered a little too quickly.

I knew it wasn't blood as soon as I saw it. There was no tangy, metallic scent in the air. "Paint, I think."

I folded my arms over my stomach, reeling for some form of comfort. Not only had someone broken into the clinic, they'd done it for the sole purpose of leaving me a message.

This had to be from whoever killed Polly and Justin. But how did they know I was snooping around and poking my nose where it didn't belong?

The only person I'd vaguely confided in was Skeeter, and I didn't think this was him. I'd talked with Bree, but again, there was no way my pixie tech did this.

That could mean only one thing.

The real killer was onto me.

Goosebumps spread over my skin, and I stifled a gasp. Beside me, the detective's eyes darted between me and the wall.

His features darkened. "Why is someone threatening you, Miss Pane?"

My leg trembled, and I turned toward the coffee machine to hide the emotions I knew were probably flashing across my face.

Picking up a fresh mug, I filled it to the top while I worked to regain control of my emotions. I handed it to Ryder and gestured for him to sit at the small table in the corner.

It was time to tell the detective everything.

CHAPTER TWENTY-TWO

R yder was incredibly calm as he listened to me recount my recent adventures—even when I got to the part about going into Polly's house and finding the notebook.

For obvious reasons, I left out the part where I used vamp mind control on one of his officers and simply told him I walked in after the young man's shift was finished. There was no need to get anyone else in trouble for my own questionable choices.

As carefully as I could, I explained the dates in the notebook and every other detail that followed in my haphazard attempts to make sense of what happened. It was odd how much a person could uncover in such a short amount of time, especially when that person was as determined as I was.

By the time I got to the part about the yoga class, I was

out of breath and getting ready for a life sentence. Ryder surprised me, and to my utter shock, after I finished spilling my guts, I remained uncuffed and not locked behind bars.

He did give me a scolding about interfering with police business and mentioned that he should probably put it on record that I broke into an active crime scene. But for the most part, he was fairly understanding. He even thanked me for the bizarre hints Elvis had been dropping and said he'd communicate the star pattern discovery to the other police jurisdictions working the robbery cases.

I promised to drop the notebook off first thing in the morning so his team could follow up on it since I figured it should be in his hands now that I'd laid everything out in the open. And while Ryder couldn't confirm if my theories had a leg to stand on—which was fair because I wasn't even fully convinced they made any rational sense—he did promise to follow up.

Before leaving me alone in the clinic, he issued a stern warning that if I came across anything else, I was to call him immediately instead of running headfirst into possibly dangerous situations.

No worries.

After tonight, I was done playing detective. He could keep his job as far as I was concerned.

I dipped a sponge into a mixture of paint thinner and water and rubbed out the remaining residue of paint from the wall. With Ryder gone, my emotions were a whirlwind. I was no longer afraid. Now I was angry.

My blood boiled, remembering the nasty message on the

wall. Someone—someone dangerous—had broken into my place of business and quite literally defiled it. I'd worked my butt off to make the clinic a welcoming place for my clients, and I hated that the stench of fear was attached to it. This was my second home, my baby, my sanctuary.

Biceps aching, I scrubbed until the white paint started to peel, then stepped back to inspect my work. There was a slight tinge of pink where the words had been, but I'd gotten rid of the majority of it. A fresh coat of paint would make it as good as new again, and I made a note to stop by the hardware store on the way home and pick a can up.

I tidied up the exam rooms, getting them ready for next week when we planned to reopen, then dropped into the swivel chair at the front desk and powered up the main computer. As much as I dreaded what came next, there was no choice left. The clinic was busier than ever, and our voicemail was full just from the people wanting to book appointments.

Bree and I couldn't handle this place on our own; I needed to replace Justin, and I needed to do it fast. The influx of calls wasn't letting up, and I refused to risk running Bree into the ground—she was incredible at her job, and I had come to think of the pixie as a friend. Besides, with another person on the team, I could afford to take a day off here and there, which I desperately needed.

The laptop came to life with a soft whir, and I opened up a few tabs of job search websites. As I scrolled through the pages, I noted the names of possible candidates so I could run them by Bree before calling people in for interviews.

Minutes ticked by, and before I knew it, the sun was rising. Pressing my palm to my mouth, I stifled a yawn and pushed aside the notepad I'd been writing in. Underneath it, a crumpled piece of paper fell to the floor.

Picking it up, I found it was one of Bree's scratch papers she doodled on while manning the front desk. I often saw her scribbling on pieces of paper when she answered phones, a habit I didn't think she even realized she had. I smoothed out the crinkled paper on the desk to admire the drawings.

"Wow. She's pretty good."

Bree's sketches were closer to raw pieces of art rather than the simple scribbled stick figures most of us made while absentmindedly doodling. There was a drawing of a small cottage on the riverside, the pen strokes detailed and precise. Beneath it, a portrait of a frowning Labradoodle made me giggle. I recognized that dog instantly, and Bree had captured his perma-frown perfectly. Beside the dog portrait was a sketch of a night sky glittering with stars.

Each drawing was stunning in its own right, and I found myself unable to look away. My gaze drifted over each one, mesmerized by the attention to detail. When I looked closer at the night sky, I leaned in. Stars. Elvis's favorite squawk rang out in my head, and I was immediately back in my house, staring at the map on the wall with the robbery locations.

You promised Ryder you wouldn't do anything else to hinder the investigation, I reminded myself with a shake of my head.

Technically, the robberies weren't the investigation he'd warned me to stay away from...

And as hard as I tried, I couldn't get my thoughts off Tristan Drummond. Dusty's son stuck in my mind, and while I couldn't place my finger on what it was, I knew there was something about him that bothered me.

Ignoring the warnings in my mind that sounded suspiciously like Ryder Wolff's voice, I turned my attention back to the laptop and opened a fresh tab, typing Tristan's name into the search bar before I lost my nerve. After checking a few of his social media profiles, all of which had way too many selfies for my personal taste, I started down the rabbit hole of pulling up everything I could relevant to his name.

Two hours and one blood box later, I knew more about Tristan Drummond than I did about my own mother. For someone young enough that he still couldn't legally drink in some countries, Tristan sure had a long resume.

After barely graduating from high school, the kid bounced from job to job, never settling into a stable career. I found rants online from customers who'd dealt with him on three different occasions and at three different restaurants. I didn't know him personally, but it appeared the food industry was not Tristan's calling. Neither was bartending nor his short stint as a used car salesman a few towns over.

I followed Tristan's digital footprints to a makeshift website, clicking on it without a second thought. As the site loaded, I was greeted with a picture of Tristan smiling from ear to ear, his pearly whites sparkling and on full display. Beneath the image were the words, "If it's broken, I'll fix it."

I cringed and kept scrolling, only to find more of the same. It seemed Tristan was trying to promote himself as some sort of handyman, able to take on any job the client needed doing.

An image of his mother's wreck of a front yard popped into my mind, and I immediately felt sorry for whoever hired him. Continuing to scroll, I noticed a button that said "Work done" and clicked it.

A sad, mostly empty page opened with a few random places listed on it. I read through each one, pulling them up on separate tabs. Most were small stores in different towns, there were a few banks listed—two of which had closed down—and the rest were names of other businesses I couldn't find anywhere on the internet. My attention snapped to a familiar name: the Grab 'n Go convenience store.

Hmm.

The first thing that struck me as odd was that Tristan had listed the convenience store here when the website was to promote his self-proclaimed handyman skills. From what I'd gathered in my brief conversation with Calli Burr, Tristan had helped out at the store. He hadn't fixed anything. Unless he was referring to Tim's old warehouse. *Strange.* I hadn't realized he'd actually started working on the place, but perhaps I was mistaken.

The second thing I couldn't quite place was why the names on the list seemed vaguely familiar. It was as though I had seen them all somewhere before, but I couldn't quite put my finger on where. I jotted them all down on the same paper I'd written the vet tech candidates on and tucked them into my purse.

Deciding to head home for the day, I shut down the computer and locked up the clinic. The street was buzzing with activity despite the early hour, and it took me twice as long to reach the hardware store as it normally would. I was stopped for polite small talk by four other business owners and one out-of-town tourist couple who needed directions to the Honeybee Bakery.

When I saw the hand-painted sign for the hardware store on the corner, I all but jogged toward it, eager to get off the main street before I was stopped again. I ducked into the store, waved hello to Seb, the owner, and headed straight to the paint section.

"Huh," I said to no one in particular. "There are fifteen shades of white, and they all look the same!"

"You need some help over there?" Seb yelled from the front register.

I waved him off. "Not yet, but I'll let you know! Trying to figure out if I need the Arctic White or Bunny Hop White."

"Bunny Hop has yellow undertones," he offered.

I had no clue what that meant. Continuing to stare at the paint samples, all of which blended together, I cocked my head to the right and left, picturing the shade of white in the clinic. I groaned and closed my eyes, randomly choosing a can. As I walked to the register, the numbers on the bottom of the can caught my eye, and I paused.

"Of course!" I shouted.

Not far from me, Seb yelled back, "What was that?"

"Talking to myself," I told him, reaching into my purse to yank out the piece of paper I'd scribbled on earlier.

Holding it in my left hand, I held my phone in my right and scrolled through the images in my gallery. When I reached the pictures I'd taken of Skeeter's notes on Polly's book, my eyes bulged.

"No way…" I whispered.

"Did you say something?"

Ignoring Seb, I continued to study the two lists side by side. On one side were the locations of the robberies in the order they'd happened, and on the other were the places Tristan had supposedly fixed up.

I swallowed hard.

The two lists were nearly identical.

CHAPTER TWENTY-THREE

Byrd curled up on the couch beside me, his tiny snores filling the living room. After I separated him and Elvis, placing the parrot in his cage and out of sight in my bedroom, the bat was so tired from their playtime that he fell asleep instantly. I couldn't help but smile, watching him relax on the velvety soft fabric.

At the clinic, Byrd kept mainly to himself, occasionally poking out from his many hiding spots to visit the occasional animal. But our patients were only passing through and left no time for Byrd to play with them. Having Elvis here was exciting for the tiny bat, a built-in companion to cause havoc with while I was away.

His tiny fingers twitched, and he covered his nose with his wings, falling deeper into slumber. He was such a sweet little guy. Most of the time.

While Byrd napped, my thoughts returned to the client list on Tristan's obscure website. There was no way I could easily check if he had any connection to the robbed businesses outside of Bluejay Falls, and I wouldn't put it past Tristan to lie about working at the ones he'd listed just to puff up his résumé, but still. My gut told me there was something there.

"I should call Ryder," I told Byrd.

The bat chittered in his sleep and completely covered his face with his wings. *Point taken.*

I stretched out, then slowly stood from the couch so I didn't disturb Byrd, and walked to the bathroom. Catching sight of my reflection, I gasped. Not because vamps didn't have one; that was just another myth humans told their children to scare them.

No, what horrified me was how tired I looked. Between the lack of sleep, possible malnutrition, and the nerves that constantly had me on edge, I looked undead.

Letting the water run, I ran my hands under the ice-cold stream and patted my cheeks. Giving my curly hair a tousle, I gathered it at the nape of my neck with a scrunchie, dabbed on some concealer, and put on a couple strokes of mascara.

I still looked pale, but at least now I could fool people if I kept them at a distance. I thanked my lucky stars my mom couldn't see me now. She'd be absolutely horrified.

Glancing at my watch, I made sure I didn't miss our scheduled call, so I didn't have to hear about it for the next week, and stepped into the bedroom. Elvis was being awfully quiet, so I moved to check on him.

As I moved toward the cage, I wondered for the tenth time why Tristan had listed the Burr's warehouse on his website. When Skeeter and I had seen it, it was so run down it would have been a public safety issue. Why try to promote your handyman skills with that monstrosity?

"Why the warehouse?" I growled out loud, peeking under the cage cover to find Elvis was sleeping.

Leaving the room, I walked down the hallway. A breeze floated through an open window in the kitchen, and the door to the tiny pantry room slammed shut. I jumped in surprise, my head swiveling to face the sound. As my eyes zeroed in on the pantry, a memory of another small room came to mind.

Hadn't Calli Burr mentioned the warehouse having a panic room?

"Why do you care? Let the detective handle this. He's the expert!" I muttered.

It was none of my business what Tristan was up to or how he was connected to the robberies. Yet there was something odd about all of it, and now that the puzzle was in my head, I couldn't let it go.

If he was somehow connected to the robberies—or if he was solely responsible for them—he would need somewhere to hide his loot. You couldn't very well walk hundreds of thousands of stolen dollars into a bank and open an account.

I doubted Tristan would be foolish enough to keep the money at home, and I didn't think Dusty knew anything about it if he was involved. Not after the way she doted on her perfect son.

That meant Tristan needed a hiding spot. One no one would know about and one that was secure enough to keep his stolen cash.

A place like a panic room no one had used in decades.

Perhaps that was why Tristan had offered to fix up the warehouse for the Burrs, to get access to that room to hide his treasure.

I raked my fingers through my hair, messing it up again. The theory was a stretch at best, yet it felt like I was onto a big lead.

Casting a quick glance at Byrd, I grabbed my jacket and headed for the front door. Locking up behind me, I dialed Ryder's number, only to get his voicemail again.

The beep sounded, and I sucked in a breath, saying, "Hi, Detective. Lia again. Listen, I have a hunch. Can you meet me at the docks? I'll text you the address. Thanks."

Taking long strides, I walked to the car and got in, starting the ignition. Time to test out my theory.

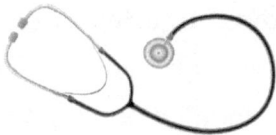

A DESERTED BOAT rocked against the dock as I walked down the familiar path to the abandoned warehouse. The steady thump echoed through the area, emphasizing how alone I was here. From the looks of it, if there were other people around, they were playing the world's most advanced game of hide-and-go-shriek, because I couldn't see any signs of life.

Great, I thought. *Way to listen to the detective and stay out of possibly dangerous situations.*

In my defense, I highly doubted my theory had any weight to it. Even if Tristan was using the warehouse to stash stolen money, what were the chances he'd be here now? And why continue to use it after the Burrs sold the place? He had no way of knowing if the new owner had plans for the decrepit space.

I calmed myself further with a reminder that Ryder would probably get my message soon and would probably storm down to the docks to make sure I didn't stumble over another dead body. So there. I wasn't alone, after all. At least I wouldn't be soon.

Up ahead, I spotted the narrow passage between buildings, and I squeezed through it. Gravel and glass crunched under my feet as I made the short walk from the dock to the front entrance of the warehouse. A shiver ran down my body at the sight of the warehouse looming larger than life before me, making me question my decision to come here. Back home, the theory seemed solid, but now that I was here, I was doubting myself.

I should call Ryder back and tell him not to bother. The last thing I wanted was to drag the detective away from police work to come chase down my poorly thought-out ideas. I pulled out my phone, and a text message popped up on the screen.

"Be there soon."

Rolling my eyes, I put the phone back in my pocket. I might as well wait for him now. Stepping back, I studied the building. The sun overhead was casting an ominous shadow over the broken-down facade. Tristan had better hope no one checked this place to gauge his skills as a handyman.

With the sun beating down on my skin, sweat beaded on my forehead. I removed my jacket but quickly changed my mind when I remembered I hadn't applied sunscreen to my arms and was wearing a short-sleeve shirt underneath. If I stayed out here much longer, I'd boil to death.

Searching over my shoulder for Ryder, I waited another five minutes before the searing sunshine forced me to step inside. I hovered in the doorway for what felt like forever, then slid further in.

Step by step, I reworked the path Skeeter and I made through the warehouse during our visit, thinking it was the safest bet since nothing had impaled us. Shattered windows cast slivers of light throughout the depressing space. I studied the floor as I walked, but as far as I could tell, there was no basement in the warehouse. To my right, the stairs of death I'd spotted before called my name, and it took everything I had to ignore it.

Wait for Ryder.

I looked toward the entrance. "Where are you, Ryder?"

A scuffing sound echoed through the cavernous space of the warehouse and sent a full-body chill through me. Curiosity won over logic, and with cautious steps, I traced the source of the noise to the rear of the warehouse, where a half-erected wall obstructed my view. Peering over the makeshift barrier, I glimpsed a long corridor stretching out before me, its length punctuated by a few nondescript doors on either side.

Pausing to assess my surroundings, I hesitated before taking another step. Gathering my courage, I skirted around the half-wall, careful not to disturb the eerie silence that enveloped the warehouse.

I tiptoed down the corridor until I reached for the handle of the first door I came to. With a silent prayer, I turned the knob, and the door swung open to reveal an empty room. Its boring interior was unfurnished, save for a lone rusty metal stool leaning against the peeling walls.

Undeterred by the lame climax to this misadventure, I proceeded to the next door, anticipation mingling with fear in my chest. This time, the door resisted my efforts, its hinges groaning in protest as I pushed against the metal. With a final shove from my shoulder, the door relented, revealing yet another vacant room. Disappointment washed over me.

My boot caught on a hard object on the ground, and I tripped, my ankle rolling under me. Using my hands to break my fall, I slammed to the floor, wincing as the cement scraped the soft part of my palms. Brushing away dirt, I stood up and looked at what had tripped me—the world's biggest rusty bolt. I kicked it with my foot, and it rolled into a crevice near the wall. *Safety first, kids.*

The deep crack in the wall caught my attention. Unlike the other cracks in the concrete, this one was painfully straight and ran all the way to the floor.

I traced its shape with my finger. "Weird."

As my palm grazed the rough surface of the wall, a small notch scraped against my skin, and I stopped. Bringing my face closer, I used my fingers to pull it up, my ears perking as a loud creak emerged from behind the wall.

"No way," I whispered, watching in awe as the wall opened up before me.

This must be the panic room.

Not giving myself a chance to reconsider, I walked into the panic room, swinging the door wide. It hit the wall with a crash, bouncing back toward me. Jumping out of the way before it could ram me in the back, the door closed tight.

My eyes slid around the panic room, taking in the wall-to-wall shelving that reached all the way to the ceiling. Unlike the rest of the warehouse, this area had undergone a recent transformation, evidenced by the sturdy steel beams anchoring each corner and the freshly laid cement underfoot.

Within this fortified shelter, the shelves stood securely affixed to the walls with metal braces, ensuring their stability under the worst of natural disasters. This structure was a crucial safeguard, which made sense given the valuable cargo packed tight on the shelves—row after row of meticulously arranged bundles of cash.

A loud scraping sound echoed from behind me, and I spun around to face the source of the noise.

My eyes widened as my gaze landed on the person standing in the middle of the panic room. "You're not Tristan."

CHAPTER TWENTY-FOUR

I stood frozen, my shock palpable, as I tried to make sense of the scene in front of me.

Bess Case, her expression a mixture of panic and uncertainty, stood before me like a deer caught in headlights. Her mouth moved soundlessly, resembling a fish gasping for air as she struggled to find the right words to respond to my accusatory glare.

In that tense moment, the truth hung heavy in the air, undeniable. There, in her grasp, lay a substantial pile of cash that I knew without a doubt had been stolen. Bess's guilt was as plain as day, written in the trembling of her fingers as they death-gripped her ill-gotten gains.

Silence enveloped us, broken only by the ticking of the clock on the wall, each passing second somehow amplifying the weight of the revelation. There was no need for words;

the evidence spoke volumes. Bess and I shared a knowing glance, acknowledging what was going on here.

Licking my lips and clearing my throat, I asked, "Bess? What are you doing here?"

"I could ask you the same question," she retorted defensively.

"It's a long story," I said. "Bess, please tell me this isn't what it looks like."

Justin's sister bristled, her fingers wrapping tighter over the bundle in her hands. She turned around and placed it on a shelf next to the others, her back rigid.

"How did you find the warehouse?" she asked. "And this room. No one knows it's here."

"I talked to the original owners. And it's listed on Tristan's website."

"Idiot!" she spat. "I told that worthless moron to take the stupid site down. He was supposed to do it ages ago. Word of advice… Lia, right? Never trust a man to do a job you can handle yourself. Especially not a cute one."

Slow as molasses, the pieces came together in my head. The girlfriend Dusty had mentioned when I'd first spoken to her about her son, the date Bess had been late for… She and Tristan were a thing.

I looked past her shoulder at the rows of neatly counted money. Not just a regular couple, either; they were a modern-day Bonnie and Clyde, from the looks of it.

I bit my bottom lip, thinking it over. "Whose idea was it to start robbing small businesses?"

"Oh, don't look at me!" She sniffed, almost indignant.

"Tristan had his half-cocked operation going long before I came along."

It all made sense now. The sheer number of places he'd worked wasn't because of a lack of commitment. Tristan had been using his position as a part-time employee to scope out the places before he took them for everything they had. It was a nasty plan and one that had hurt a lot of people, robbing owners of their livelihood. Had Bess known what she was signing up for when she started dating the despicable thief?

She picked up another stack and fanned it with her finger.

Well, that answered that question.

My stomach turned in disgust. "But you still stuck with him after you found out what he was doing?"

Bess laughed, the sound like nails on a chalkboard. I cringed, internally recoiling from her.

"Honey, please. Look around you!" She opened her arms wide and turned to face me. "All of this wouldn't be here without me. Before I came along, Tristan was running his sad little schemes with no direction and no planning. Thanks to me, we have enough to retire somewhere nice and warm once we sell this heap of junk alone."

"You're the anonymous buyer?"

She shrugged. "Not so anonymous anymore, I suppose."

What was happening here? I'd known the robberies weren't the doing of a single person, but never in my wildest dreams had I thought Justin's sister was one of them. To be frank, I hadn't even fully believed my theory about Tristan until right that very second.

What could make two people go to such an extent for years? And had they gotten away with it for so long? The brief conversation I'd had with Tristan didn't paint him as a genius capable of thwarting the police across multiple towns.

Bess must be the brains behind the operation.

I studied her every move, my thoughts circling back to Justin. "I don't understand. Your brother... Did you kill him?"

A storm gathered in her eyes, and she looked down at her feet, refusing to meet my gaze. Her fingers curled into tight fists, knuckles white and angry. When she finally looked up, I stumbled back in shock. It wasn't sadness I saw in Bess's features; it was white-hot rage.

"Justin was a righteous, self-centered fool," she seethed. "I told him to leave me alone. To leave Tristan alone. But no, he kept digging. That was my brother for you. Always sticking his nose where it didn't belong."

"And you killed him for it?" My voice shook.

She wiggled an index finger back and forth. "*I* didn't do anything. All I did was agree to meet him. To talk."

Tristan, then. The femme fatale had gotten her boyfriend to do her dirty bidding. If Bess was trying to convince me she hadn't wanted her brother gone, she was failing miserably. I didn't buy a word coming out of her mouth.

My legs trembled, and I battled the urge to pull out my

phone and check on the detective. What was taking him so long? He should've been here already.

I flicked my eyes to the walls in the panic room, then back to Bess. "This looks like it was recently remodeled," I noted, deciding I needed to keep her busy talking while I figured out how to get away from her.

"One good thing Tristan did," she answered. "When he first pitched the idea of buying the warehouse, I thought it was a dumb play. Until he told me about the panic room. It's the perfect hiding spot, don't you think? No one would even know to look here."

I thought back to the detective. Shoot.

Finding the panic room had been purely accidental on my part, so I doubted Ryder would think to check in here. With the door closed, it was nearly impossible to distinguish the room from the wall, and Ryder didn't know the panic room even existed. I side-eyed the walls again. Twenty bucks said they were soundproof.

But what could Bess do, really? It was only the two of us here, and worst-case scenario, I'd go a bit batty, freak her out, and hope it bought me enough time to get away. Then I could go find Ryder and tell him everything Bess had told me.

"I hate to do this, truly, but you leave me no choice," Bess said.

Turning my head back toward Bess, my mouth went dry, and my heart lodged itself into my throat. I was staring straight into the barrel of the gun she had pointed at me.

Okay... *Now what?*

I lifted my hands up high, palms out—the universal sign of surrender. Sweat slid down my brow and trickled into my eyes, causing them to burn like a witch. I squinted and tried to breathe through the panic that was seizing my lungs.

Even if I managed to transform faster than I ever had before, which was a big if, I still wouldn't be fast enough to beat a flying bullet. To top it off, I had no idea how good a shot Bess was, and knowing my luck, she'd shoot my adorable bat butt for target practice.

I could try compulsion, but I'd have to be close enough to capture her full attention, and something told me Bess wasn't interested in getting up close and personal with me.

She waved the gun lightly and warned, "Whatever you're thinking, don't."

My only chance of surviving this was to keep her talking. Against my better judgment, I unlocked my clenched jaw.

"Is that what your boyfriend told Justin before he killed him, too?" I asked. "Were you there when he stuffed your brother's body behind the dumpster? Did you make sure to supervise him to make sure he did the job right?"

Bess seethed. I'd hit a nerve.

"Don't pretend to know anything about me or my brother. Justin had it coming."

"Did Polly?"

The gun dipped slightly as Bess considered my question. Her eyes were unfocused, a slight shine making them appear to be made of glass, and her brow creased as she asked, "Who?"

"Polly Ester," I replied. "The woman you killed because she found out about your little ring of robberies? Tristan's mother's neighbor?"

Bess's confusion gave me my answer.

"You had no idea he killed her, did you?"

Shaking, Bess's lips formed a tight, white line, and she jabbed the barrel of the gun toward my head.

"Enough! I don't care about some random neighbor. If Tristan got rid of her, it's because she was in the way." She snapped her teeth together. "Like you. Now move over there!"

As she pointed at the corner of the panic room, I knew my days—more like minutes—were numbered. No one asked you to back into a corner unless it was going to be the last place you'd see before they killed you. My steps were unsteady as I slowly walked to where Bess pointed with my chin lifted high.

Head spinning, I tried to think of a plan, but nothing came to mind. My breath caught, and for a second, I felt like I was choking. Chest tight, I took another step, the rush of my blood pulsing in my veins, pounding in my ringing ears.

An idea popped into my head, and I clung to it like a lifeline. I calmed my ragged breaths as I stood stock still.

Behind me, Bess screeched, "Move!"

Her footsteps moved toward me, and as she neared, I threw out my arm and swiped at the bundles of money on the shelf nearest me. The stacks flew off the shelf and hit the floor one by one, their thudding numbed by the sound-proofing under the flooring.

"What did you do that for?" Bess snarled.

She couldn't help herself and bent to pick up the cash. I took my chance. Using my right leg, I kicked at her shoulder, knocking her to her butt. Bess yelped and waved the gun at me, but her aim was off now. It didn't help that she still held the armful of money stacks that she refused to let go of. Spinning on my heel, I tried to remember the one self-defense class I'd taken when I was younger and kicked my leg out on the twist.

I missed. Obviously.

Instead of hitting Bess's arm that held the gun, I slammed my boot into another shelf and sent more money toppling over. On the floor, Bess shrieked in frustration, and despite my failed karate move, I seemed to have distracted her long enough to give me a sliver of a chance to escape.

I leaped over Justin's sister and rushed for the door. My fingers clawed around the invisible frame as I frantically searched for a similar latch to the one on the outside of the door. Trembling, I searched the wall until I felt a ridge, then pulled with all my might.

The door swung open, and I tumbled out of the panic room, exhaling with pure relief. My foot caught on the uneven ground, and I tripped, careening forward but catching myself just before I face-planted on the warehouse floor.

Not waiting around to see if Bess was going to chase

after me, I took off like a bat out of Hades. Her footsteps echoed at my back, and I turned my head to glance over my shoulder. Behind me, Bess gave chase but stopped at the entrance to the panic room. Her attention focused on something down the corridor.

My blood turned to ice at Bess's smirk, and a moment later, a hard object slammed into the side of my skull. Unbearable pain surged through my body, and my vision swam. I fought to stay conscious and upright, but it was no use. In seconds, my body hit the concrete with a heavy thud.

The world blurred, and my vision turned dark as unconsciousness claimed me.

CHAPTER TWENTY-FIVE

My vision came in and out of focus, blurring at the edges each time, like an old film reel. Black dots swam in the narrow space in front of my face. I struggled to keep my heavy lids open, feeling as if they were weighed down by lead. Muffled voices drifted around me, distant and indistinct, as if they were echoing through a long tunnel. Despite my best efforts, I couldn't make out a single word.

The persistent ringing in my ear started to subside, and I drew in one shaky breath after another. As I twisted on my side, attempting to orient myself, a sharp pain shot through my neck like a lightning bolt. I doubled over in agony.

What happened back there? How had I injured myself? Memories flickered like candles in my foggy brain. I strained to piece together the events leading up to this moment, but they remained stubbornly out of reach.

"Make sure the ropes hold," a disembodied voice instructed.

"I already checked them twice." This voice sounded familiar, but I couldn't place it. "She's not going anywhere."

The first person, a male, spoke again, but I didn't catch what he said. A finger pressed under my chin and tilted my head back. The bells in my ears sounded an alarm, and I groaned, choking on the bile in my throat.

I blinked hard, finally chasing away my blurred vision, just in time to see Bess come into focus in front of me.

"She's alive. Good."

"This is dumb," the man said from behind her. "You should have let me finish her off before she came to."

Bess growled. "Like you finished off your mom's neighbor?"

Ah. Tristan.

Of course. I should have known the lap dog wouldn't be too far from Bess. It was foolish of me not to check for him before. Now, I was paying the price for my stupidity. Tied up in a room no one even knew existed, with two killers looming over me. The worst part was that the blow to my head had caused a monstrous migraine that was making it impossible for me to even attempt to use my vamp abilities.

"How did you know about that?" Tristan grumbled.

"Who cares?" Bess snapped, yanking hard on the ropes around my wrists and ankles again. She shoved her hands under my arms, hauling me up and forcing me to sit with my back against a wall. "Why did you kill her? You should have talked to me before taking a risk like that!"

"Polly figured it out. I don't know how, but she figured it out, and she told your brother."

Making eye contact with me for the first time since I came to, Bess rolled her eyes as though we were two best friends complaining about loser boyfriends over drinks.

Girl, I am not your bestie. She could go suck a stake, for all I cared.

"She didn't tell my brother anything," Bess scoffed, exhaustion heavy in her voice. "That nosy son of a gun put two and two together on his own. He went on and on about a talking parrot. He figured it out because of a freaking bird."

Elvis. Justin must have heard Elvis squawking about the robberies and put two and two together. I swallowed the bile that threatened to choke me.

How had poor Justin felt knowing his own sister would rather watch him die than come clean for the robberies? The thought made me grateful for my parents. People didn't choose their family, and I'd lucked out big time in that category, unlike Justin, who'd gotten this sad sack for a sister.

And to think Bess had actually tried to paint him in a bad light when I'd come asking questions. Justin might have had a gambling problem, but this woman was a monster through and through. To kill your own family for money... What a greedy coward. I shifted in my seat, my back scraping against the roughness of the wall. The ropes caught a loose nail, and I hid my delighted surprise.

Head in the game, Lia. Get out. Get out now!

I looked at Bess through wet lashes. "I told the police

everything I know. If anything happens to me, they'll know it was you."

"I told you we should have gotten it over with and got out of town," Tristan snarled.

"Quiet!" Bess roared. "She's bluffing. She didn't even know it was me until she showed up here."

A clarity formed in my brain as the fog from the blow to my skull began to lift. *If I can split them up, I have a shot.*

I rolled my shoulders, uncurling my spine to sit taller so I could see Tristan. "But I knew it was you," I told him.

The self-assured grin he sported faltered.

"The police might not know about Bess, but they certainly have your name. In fact, they're probably questioning your mother as we speak. She's a chatty one, isn't she?" I tore my gaze from him, turning back to Bess. "How long do you think it'll be until she tells them who Tristan is dating?"

I saw the wheels turning in Bess's head as she registered what I said. Even if they got rid of me, there was no way out for them. Well, technically, there was, but they didn't know that. I needed to push this further, get them to turn on each other. The harder I concentrated, the harder my head pounded. This would be so much easier if I could just compel Bess to untie me.

Wiggling my wrists, I worked to untie the bindings behind my back, careful not to move too much. I could feel them loosen, but there still wasn't enough give for me to slip my hands out. Even if I could, what then? I was outnumbered and outgunned. Without my abilities, there was no way I could overpower both Bess and Tristan.

Think, Lia!

Struggling to get free, I focused my efforts on the couple. My best bet was to keep them arguing long enough to come up with a plan, or at least until my head cleared enough that I could attempt to transform.

I cleared my throat. "I hope you two have a getaway plan. You're going to need it."

"Shut up!" Tristan roared.

It was the first time I'd seen him lose his cool, and it terrified me. His face contorted, a vein swelling in his otherwise smooth forehead. Eyes narrowed, he walked toward me, stalking me like a predator. I wondered if Dusty knew what a monster her son truly was.

Tristan's face reddened as he leaned down over me. "You can't talk your way out of this."

I forced a confident laugh. "Oh, I know. Trust me, I get this is it for me. But I figured Bess deserves to know who she tied herself to." My eyes flicked to Justin's sister. "Did you know I found you because of a secret notebook Polly kept? The one I'm willing to bet your boyfriend killed her over."

A flash of distrust lit in Bess's eyes.

Keep going.

"The funny thing is, there was a lot of interesting information in it," I lied. "Not just everything Polly found out about your little robberies. I have to hand it to her. She was very detail-oriented. It all makes so much sense."

"I thought I told you to shut up!" Tristan yelled.

He raised his arm, ready to strike me, but Bess stopped him. "Let her talk."

I've got you.

My mind raced as I tried to formulate the best lie to get them arguing. Bess and Tristan were a pack, a team of feral creatures who stuck together not out of love but necessity. The way Bess had spoken of her boyfriend earlier told me as much. My work with the werewolves in our town taught me a lot about pack behavior. I racked my brain for the answer. What was the best way to put a gap between pack members?

I eyed Bess, and the answer came to me with perfect clarity. Question their alpha authority.

"Have you ever asked your boyfriend what he planned to do with all the money?" I asked. "After your last heist, I mean."

Bess's brow furrowed.

"Didn't think so. Polly knew, though," I snorted. "Tristan was never going to stay with you, Bess. You were a patsy. Someone to blame the entire thing on so he could run off with the cash. He had a place waiting for him in Canada, off the grid, so no one could find him. He was going to leave you in the dust, and Polly found out."

"She's lying!" Tristan argued, his voice rising. "I would never do that, babe!"

He tried to come closer, but Bess put her hand up. She was buying it... hook, line, and sinker. Bess thought of herself as the alpha, and she would have to prove her power over Tristan no matter what he said.

"It's why he killed her, Bess. Think about it," I urged. "Why else would he not tell you about it?"

The lightbulb went on in Bess's head, and she pressed her lips tightly together, her neck tensing. I tried to hide my surprise at how easily she fell for it. So much for a trusting, loving relationship. Though I supposed you could never truly trust a con artist, even if you loved them.

As Bess spun around to face off with Tristan, I yanked on the restraints. My wrists came free, and not wasting a single second, I searched the room while Bess and Tristan tried to outshout each other.

On first instinct, I started to scoot along the wall toward the door, going slow so as not to draw their attention. The incessant ringing in my ears was gone entirely, and I could focus my eyes much better now. I'd been too busy trying to distract the couple to notice my senses returning. A smile tugged at my lips.

Abandoning the stealth I had aimed for before, I reached over and untied the ropes around my ankles. Using the wall, I pushed myself into a standing position. The couple continued to bicker, not noticing my movements. In fact, by the time they noticed I wasn't on the floor anymore, I was already halfway to the door.

"Get her!" Bess shrieked.

At her command, Tristan made a beeline toward me, but my grin spread. When he was a few feet away, I spun to face him.

Opening my mouth wide, I let my fangs make a proud appearance.

"What the—"

I cut him off with a hiss, shoving my face into his. Tristan yelped, lost his balance, and teetered back. His body collided with Bess, who was rushing after him, and the two rolled over each other. Legs and arms were everywhere as they tried to untangle on the ground.

While they struggled, I leaped for the latch to open the door. A click sounded behind me, and I froze. Turning around slowly, I found myself once again facing the barrel of Bess's gun. This time, it was in Tristan's hand, though, and unlike his girlfriend, he didn't waver. The slimy son of a biscuit pulled the trigger, aiming to kill me.

Joke's on you, clown.

A loud cracking pierced the air as the gun went off. The bullet raced toward me, but I had already started the transformation. It sliced through the air beneath me as I flapped my bat wings, raising me higher until I was brushing against the ceiling.

"What is happening?" Bess shrieked.

"I don't know! Where is she?"

Working overtime, I moved my wings faster and faster, flapping those babies until I was out of breath. The sound attracted the attention of the two fools below me, and they looked up, horror registering on their faces.

Bess clung to Tristan's back like a spider monkey, screaming, "Is that a freaking bat?"

I chuckled.

"Did that bat just laugh?! It probably has rabies!" Bess sobbed.

Tristan pointed the gun at me and shot, but I was much quicker. The bullet ricocheted off a shelf and bounced back at them. Bess flinched and screamed. "Watch out, you moron! You're going to kill us."

Taking advantage of their confusion, I flew for the door, transforming into human form just as I reached it. Moving faster than lightning, I scooped my clothes off the floor, pulled on the hidden latch, and burst out of the panic room. The moment I was outside, I turned and slammed the door shut behind me.

My eyes darted left and right until I found what I needed. Grabbing the large bolt that had attacked me earlier, I threw myself at the panic room door and jammed the bolt into the latch.

Less than a heartbeat later, the door shook as Bess and Tristan attempted to open it from the other side. My chest rose and fell with heavy breaths as I leaned against the wall. Sweat poured off me in waves, and my heart raced in my ribcage.

I was alive.

Better, I had two killers trapped inside a room with only one way out.

In the distance, I heard the frantic calling of my name and realized Ryder had arrived and was searching the warehouse for me. I opened my mouth to call him over but quickly closed it again.

There were two things I had to do before the detective

found me. First, I needed to get dressed. Second, I needed to come up with a believable story about how I'd locked two armed robbers in a panic room without getting shot.

Preferably one that didn't include bat wings.

CHAPTER TWENTY-SIX

"What about the bat?" Ryder asked.

I watched two officers walk Bess and Tristan out, their hands cuffed behind their backs. As they placed them in the backseat of separate cruisers, the two glared at me through the windows with twin expressions of disbelief. The thing about the human mind was that it often tried to explain away what was right in front of it in order to choose a more believable explanation. When they'd finally been arrested, Bess and Tristan wouldn't stop going on about a rabid bat in the panic room, never once even considering I was the bat.

It made sense. The simplest explanation was often the right one... except where the supernatural world was concerned.

"It was probably a bird," I told Ryder. "Bats are nocturnal. I doubt one would venture out at this time of day."

The detective's brow creased, and his eyes narrowed on me. "Except we didn't find anything in the room. Not a bat. Not a bird." He pointed to the cruisers with his thumb. "Only those two."

I pulled at the neck of my shirt, shifting uncomfortably around. No matter what I did, I had to make sure I steered Ryder away from the bat theory. I couldn't risk the detective asking too many questions, and certainly not ones that opened up the can of worms that was the existence of the supernatural world.

Using my abilities to save my life around human beings was one thing, but blabbing about our existence to the police was the worst thing I could do as far as the paranormal council was concerned. The last guy who exposed us to someone of authority was never heard from again. The council hadn't put him to sleep with the merfishes, of course. They weren't monsters. Phil was in witness protection and had to leave his entire life behind. I didn't want to risk ending up in the same situation.

My throat felt dry as I whispered, "I wouldn't trust anything they have to say. The bird probably flew out when I opened the door."

"About that…" the detective said. "You said that while the two were preoccupied arguing and shooting at the bird, you escaped and locked them inside. Correct?"

I nodded.

"See, the thing is, Miss Pane, the suspects tell a very different story. And while I agree theirs has a fantastical twist, I'm having trouble believing you did all that on your own. Unless you have a black belt I'm unaware of."

I attempted to shrug, but my anxiety kicked into gear, and my shoulders stayed hiked up, grazing my earlobes a little. Without a neck, I probably looked even more suspicious.

Think, Lia. Think!

My brain was mush. Waving my hand nonchalantly, I forced a smile, which likely resembled a lopsided grin. "So, what?" I asked. "Are you suggesting that I have a bat side-kick that helped me?"

An image of Byrd in a superhero cape zoomed by us in my mind, and I bit the inside of my cheek before I laughed in the detective's face.

"I'm not suggesting anything of the sort." Ryder jerked his chin down the corridor and away from the police officers, dusting the panic room for prints and securing evidence.

Heart in throat, I followed the detective as he led us into one of the abandoned rooms, jutting out from the corridor. The single chair inside made it feel like an interrogation room, and I instantly regretted following him inside.

I tightened my lips into a narrow line in hopes of keeping them closed.

"I'm going to ask you a question, Miss Pane, and I need you to be frank with me."

In my head, I agreed, but in reality, I only stood there like a fool and stared.

Ryder arched one perfect brow. "You're the bat, aren't you?"

Say what now?

"Um…" I struggled to put words into sentences. "What are you talking about? That's ridiculous." My laugh was brittle and forced even to my ears.

The detective stared into space, turning something over in his mind. A strand of hair fell into his serious eyes, and I fought the ridiculous urge to brush it away.

Shaking myself back to reality, I pushed aside the inconvenient crush I was developing on the detective and waited for him to speak.

"Let's stop pretending, Miss Pane," Ryder said, still not looking at me. "Those two clowns are painting quite the unbelievable story about what happened here today."

I opened my mouth to object, but he stopped me.

"But I also know they're telling the truth. You're a vampire, Lia. Don't try to hide it, there's no point."

My world tilted wildly, and my legs trembled as I replayed his words. How did Ryder know about me? Heck, how did he know about paranormals? I sniffed the air, trying to smell his scent to confirm he was truly human, but not wanting to be obvious about it.

Confusion laced through me when all I smelled was a human male. What was happening right now?

I choked back a shocked gasp. "H-How could you know that? Humans aren't supposed to know."

The detective chuckled. "So I was correct?"

"You guessed?!" *You have got to be kidding me.* I stepped

backward, my back hitting a wall, reminding me I was trapped. "I don't understand."

Someone yelled out the detective's name, and he held up a finger, leaving me alone in the empty room. My neck swiveled as my fight-or-flight instincts kicked in.

A way out. I needed a way out.

My pulse jack-hammered, and sweat pooled at the base of my lower back as an almost feral panic set in. I took a deep breath in and out, fighting the vampire self-preservation instincts that threatened to take control.

Running from the police because a detective figured out my secret was not the answer. The council couldn't punish me for something I had no control over, could they?

I struggled to recall every interaction I'd had with Ryder since Polly died. Nope. I hadn't done anything wrong or broken any paranormal rules. I was certain of it.

Then how had he figured it out?

Heavy footfalls approached. The detective poked his head through the doorway before stepping inside. His face gave nothing away; I struggled to mimic it with little success. Unlike Ryder, I looked less like I was a fortress of secrets and more like I needed to use the bathroom.

I pinched the bridge of my nose. "So, how did you figure me out?"

Not answering, Ryder stalked across the room to close the distance between us. His green eyes stayed glued on me as he reached into the collar of his shirt and pulled out a silver chain. My stomach did a somersault. At the end of the chain was a small silver vial, an emblem etched on its round belly. I reached for it instinctively, then yanked my hand away.

"Is that…?"

"My pack's crest," Ryder said.

My jaw hit the floor. "You're a werewolf?"

As the detective nodded, the pieces snapped into place. His inhuman ability to see through my lies, the way he watched those around him like he was stalking prey, the few times I noticed him literally sniff around me. It was typical wolf behavior, and I never even realized it. Either I was losing my touch, or whatever effect Ryder had on me got in the way of my rational thinking.

No, that wasn't it.

I didn't smell the supernatural on Ryder, and that was always a telltale sign. It was how we knew who to trust. I watched the vial dangle back and forth in front of me. *Of course!*

"Who's the witch who made your invisibility charm?" I asked.

Invisibility charm was a bit of false advertising. There was no cape to drape over yourself that allowed you to hide from the world. What they excelled at, and what they were mainly used for, was to shield a supernatural's magic from prying eyes. To remove the super and make them seem completely human. That was why I couldn't smell the wolf on Ryder—he made sure no one could.

"That I cannot tell you, Miss Pane," the detective said.

I scoffed. "How long have you known what I was?"

"Since day one. You do a good job hiding it, if it makes you feel better," he offered with a smile.

"Not good enough."

Ryder chuckled. "It's my job to know these things, Lia." It wasn't the first time he'd used my first name, and I had to admit it sounded nice when he said it. "And it helps to have a clear picture of what I'm dealing with. Now that it's all out in the open, want to tell me what really happened today?"

It took the better part of an hour for me to recount every step of the day. I even backtracked and retold the story I'd already given him, this time filling it in with the parts I'd left out before. It turned out that spilling my guts wasn't as bad as I thought it would be. By the time I was done, I felt lighter, as though all the weight I'd been carrying since I'd found Polly's body had vanished instantly.

I blew out a long breath, my shoulders slumping. "And that's it. Are you going to arrest me now?"

"For what?"

"I don't know." I shrugged. "Stealing evidence, interfering with your investigation, mind-controlling one of your guys. I could go on."

Ryder's full lips melted into a smile. "When you put it that way, maybe I should," he said with a laugh. "But no. You're free to go. As far as I can tell, we still would've been chasing our tails trying to find out what these two were doing if you hadn't interfered. And Ryan could use a little mind-control if you ask me. That kid is all over the place."

"You're not mad?"

"I'm a little mad," Ryder admitted. "But I understand why you did it. Just do me a favor and come to me for help next time? Us paranormals have to stick together."

I folded my arms over my chest. "In my defense, I didn't know you were part of the 'us' until today. Why do you hide it?"

"I deal with some pretty horrible people," Ryder explained. "Both human and paranormal. For someone to know who I am and what I'm capable of, it might give them the wrong idea. And sometimes, it helps to use my abilities without anyone knowing or expecting it. Keeps the criminals on their toes."

It made sense. Werewolves were notorious hunters, and what was a police detective if not that? For Ryder to use his abilities to do his job was a brilliant play. I truly understood the need for hiding; there were times when I wished I could hide what I was, too. However, after today, I was thinking maybe I was better at being a vamp than I gave myself credit for.

"What happens now?" I asked the detective.

He rubbed his jaw, thinking about it. "Well, I'll go back to the station and process Bess and Tristan. There will be a lot of paperwork and interdepartmental red tape, but they will be going away for the rest of their lives if I have anything to do with it."

His stormy gaze rolled over me. "And you go back home. Maybe relax a little, stay out of police business for a while. That sort of thing."

"Trust me," I said, "I have no intention of getting involved in any more murders."

Ryder frowned. "Somehow, I doubt that. But it's good to hold on to hope." He started for the door, stopping to look at me over his shoulder. "Are you taking any new patients, by the way?"

Oh, no. Not another wolf. I didn't think I could handle one more alpha male, but what choice did I have? I couldn't very well say no, considering how easy Ryder was going on me.

I was about to answer when he added, "It's not me. It's my dog."

"Oh!" I exclaimed in relief. "Benny the Frenchie. Definitely! We'd love to have him."

"You might want to hold off on celebrating."

My muscles tensed. "Why? What's wrong with him?"

"Benny is a hellhound. Hope you know your way around them, because I have the hardest time finding him medical care."

"Did you say hellhound? As in *the* hellhound?"

Ryder brushed me off with a wave of his hand. "No, no. Not the big guy. Benny is one of his many litters, though, and can be difficult to manage. He's a sweet little guy, but you know, has a temper."

"Right. Sure. Bring him by next week, and we can see about getting a file started."

With that, the detective tipped his chin and walked out of the room. In the distance, I heard him ordering the officers around as they scurried to finish up what they were doing.

I made my way outside and headed for my car. Ryder was right. I needed to rest. More than that, I craved to binge movies and curl up with Byrd on the couch while Elvis chattered in the background. It was time to get back to normal life.

Or as normal as my life could be.

CHAPTER TWENTY-SEVEN

"Please make it end!" Bree's voice pierced through the cacophony, bouncing off the clinic walls. Her head shook, and the hair that had been perfectly coiffed this morning was a big, sweaty mess. The pixie waved an arm in the air, her frustrated eyes finding mine. "I will literally sell you my soul if that stops immediately."

I couldn't help but chuckle, observing the negotiation between Bree and Elvis. The parrot seemed to consider the offer, cocking his head to the side before swooping down once more. This time, he snatched a strand of Bree's newly dyed blue hair before fluttering off to perch atop another bookcase. My vet tech let out a startled shriek, to which Elvis responded with a perfect mimicry, amplifying the sound for dramatic effect.

As Elvis prepared for another round, I knew I had to

intervene before complete chaos ensued. Yet, the dynamic between these two had been the highlight of my morning. With all our patients tended to and sent home, we'd somehow managed to close early. Still, I knew I couldn't delay hiring a second vet tech from the stack of resumes on my desk much longer.

But for now, the circus unfolding before me demanded attention.

"So help me, Lia! I will quit!" Bree's threat hung in the air like a challenge.

Raising my hands in surrender, I attempted to placate the situation. "All right, all right. He's just having a bit of fun."

"I feel targeted," Bree grumbled, smoothing down her hair while shooting a narrowed glance at Elvis. I could swear I saw a mischievous glint in the bird's eyes. "When is his new owner coming to get him?"

Glancing at the clock on the wall, I replied, "Tim should be here any moment. He's a bit flighty himself. Let's hope he didn't forget."

After news got around that I was partially responsible for ridding our little town of the miscreants robbing local businesses, my phone was off the hook. I'd gotten so many calls from people wanting to know the full story I had to get a second number. Fortunately, I still answered the old number because if I hadn't, I would've missed Tim Burr's call last week. It seemed when he'd said he had a fondness for Elvis, he'd been telling me the truth.

The convenience store owner and his wife had been

talking about getting a pet for years, and he'd called to offer Elvis a home. As much as I wanted to keep Elvis, my work schedule wouldn't allow me to give him the time and regular schedule he deserved. Tim and his wife had come to the clinic to visit with Elvis, and watching the genuine affection between the three as they interacted told me all I needed to know. Elvis was going home with two people I knew would take great care of him, and Bree was about to get the autonomy of her hair back. Everything was coming up splendidly.

With Tristan and Bess behind bars and awaiting trial, the town was finally safe. Last I heard, Ryder said it might be a while before they got sentenced because of all the jurisdictions involved, but I knew it was more than that. The two had been at their scheme for years, and gathering evidence across town lines was a nightmare. No matter. The important part was that they were caught and would pay for their crimes.

I looked at Elvis, trying to gauge his mood today. Not for the first time, I wondered if he knew Polly's killers were being punished.

As if sensing my inner thoughts, Elvis turned to look at me and ground out a long squawk. "Stars above! Stars below!"

I laughed.

"That's right, buddy. Those are the only stars left now," I assured the parrot. "You're safe. We all are."

The front door creaked open, its sound reverberating down the dimly lit hallway toward us. Elvis, perched above me, let out a cheerful chirp, perfectly timed by Bree's exclamation of, "Finally."

I scooped up the carefully prepared care package I had assembled earlier—filled to the brim with provisions to sustain Elvis for a week, fresh cage liners, and an array of parrot-friendly toys—and made my way out of the room. In the background, I could hear Bree struggling to coax Elvis into his cage, her efforts punctuated by amusing noises that threatened to crack a smile on my face.

Setting the care package down by the reception desk, I smoothed back a stray strand of hair and stepped into the waiting room, fully expecting to find Tim standing there. However, to my surprise, it wasn't Tim who greeted me.

Instead, standing awkwardly amid the room's neutral decor, dressed casually in gray sweatpants and a fitted black tee, was Ryder. His disheveled hair lent him a rugged charm, and there was an undeniable aura of nonchalance about him that I couldn't help but notice despite my efforts to remain unaffected. As much as I loathed to acknowledge it, the detective undeniably looked appealing.

I felt a flutter of anticipation mixed with uncertainty at his unexpected presence. It was a stark contrast to the usual businesslike demeanor he'd exuded during our previous encounters. With a quick mental shake, I pushed aside any distracting thoughts and focused on the task at hand, bracing myself for whatever news or request Ryder might have for me.

"Ryder," I said. "I didn't expect to see you today. Is everything all right with the case?"

The detective ran a hand through his hair, smiling. "The case is good. Thank you for your help again." He glanced down at his feet. "I'm here about a different matter, actually."

I followed his gaze to the tiny bundle of energy on the ground. Benny, the French Bulldog, ran in between Ryder's legs, then settled back down to sit. He repeated the pattern several times before looking up at me.

My heart melted on the spot.

The puppy dog eyes, the spot perfectly placed on his left buttock, the way he wiggled his ears... This hellhound baby was the most adorable pup I'd seen all year.

Bending down on one knee, I held out an open palm. The puppy sniffed at my fingers, giving them a proper lick before retreating back to the safety between Ryder's legs.

"What seems to be the problem?" I asked. If he had been a shifter with a human form, I could have tried communicating with him telepathically, like I had with Bob. But hellhounds didn't have a human form, so that was a no-go.

"I..." Ryder scratched the nape of his neck. "I'm honestly not sure. We were at the dog park, and he started going bonkers. Barking, whining. He's not usually like this, so I thought I could bring him in and see what you think."

Down the hallway, Bree screeched, and a metal item clattered to the floor.

Ryder's brow creased, and he met my widening eyes. "Unless this isn't a good time."

I winced, looking over my shoulder to make sure nothing was imploding.

"Now's fine, if you don't mind waiting," I told him. "Tim's coming by to pick up Elvis shortly, and I want to make sure it goes smoothly. It's a big change for the parrot."

"The convenience store owner?" Ryder asked.

Between his legs, Benny stuck out a wet snout and sniffed the air, huffing.

I smiled and nodded slowly. "Seems he really meant it when he said he liked Elvis. Poor Dusty will never be free of the parrot," I said with a chuckle. "Tim lives right down the block from the store."

"Sadly, I think she'll be too busy with the mess her son left her with to care about anything else."

"Reporters are still all over it, huh?" I asked.

"Afraid so," Ryder replied. He bent down to pet Benny behind the ear lovingly. "But I mean it. If you want us to come back, I can be here another time."

I waved him off. "Not at all. Let's get you two settled in a room, and I'll pop in as soon as Elvis is off to his new home. Shouldn't be long now."

After leading the detective and Benny to an examination room furthest from the action, I put on a pot of coffee, promising Ryder a drink while he waited. My eyes stayed glued to the front door as I started a file for our newest patient. While I didn't think there was anything seriously wrong with the Frenchie, it was best to give him a full checkup.

Ryder was right; it was odd how the dog had behaved, and from my limited knowledge of hellhounds, they weren't normally prone to sudden changes in attitude.

Staying calm in tough situations was part of the breed's character, a gene embedded in their paranormal DNA to account for the job they had. You had to keep a cool head to herd the dead.

As I waited for Tim's arrival, the office felt unusually quiet, the air heavy with anticipation. Restless, I scanned the applications for vet techs spread out on the desk before me. Each resume seemed to blur into the next, but something caught my eye—smiley faces drawn in pink marker adorned a handful of them. Bree had left her subtle mark, a clear indication of her preferences. I smiled, appreciating her additions.

However, my thoughts quickly turned sour as I thought about Justin's tragedy. The memory of his funeral, just a week ago, still weighed heavily on me. Justin's untimely death had shaken our small veterinary clinic to its core, leaving a void that seemed impossible to fill. Bree's input on the hiring process suddenly carried a deeper significance; after all, she had been here when I'd found Justin. She deserved to have a say about who we brought in next.

The mere mention of the vet tech position stirred up a whirlwind of emotions within me. Despite my best efforts to move forward, Justin's absence lingered like a shadow, a constant reminder of what had occurred so close to home. I couldn't shake the feeling of foreboding that seemed to cling to every corner, every alleyway.

Even now, as I sat in the quiet of the office, I found myself glancing over my shoulder, instinctively checking the alley outside—a futile gesture, perhaps, but one that had become a ritual these last few weeks. The sense of vulnerability that had gripped me since Justin's passing refused to dissipate, and I wasn't sure why I couldn't let it go.

Bree's subtle message conveyed through those pink smiley faces, served as a reminder that life must inevitably go on. Or anything equally encouraging that I was certain the pixie would say if she was privy to my inner thoughts. Knowing her, she'd have quite a bit to say about those. My head was a hot mess express train most days.

With a heavy heart, I returned my focus to the task at hand, knowing that although Justin's absence would be keenly missed, I would have to make decisions in the coming days that would shape the clinic's future.

Adding my own smiley faces to a few potential candidates, I tucked the applications in a drawer and stepped back. My heel caught a bump on the ground, and I toppled over, hip slamming into the desk as I wobbled to right my balance. The hit sent a ripple of pain down my side, and I yelped, rubbing it to numb the area. My eyes narrowed, scanning the foot of the desk for the obstruction.

"What in the…"

I bent down and reached toward the carry-on suitcase lying on the floor, pulling it out slowly. The zipper was undone, and I carefully pulled up the front flap of the suitcase. In the bag, curled amid what looked to be three different baby blankets, was Byrd. The bat's tiny head was hidden under a wing, and I could hear his tiny snores rise, his chest bobbing with sleep.

With a grin on my face, I closed the flap and pushed the suitcase back under the desk.

"Bree!" I yelled out into the hallway. "What's Byrd doing in a suitcase?"

The pixie popped her head out from a doorway, shockingly not the one I'd left her in. "Oh! I forgot to warn you. He hitched a ride home with me last night and I had nothing else to transport him back in." From inside the exam room, Elvis squawked, and Bree rolled her eyes. "I think he likes it there, though. We should probably leave it here at the office for him."

The front door swung open again before I could reply about the fact that we already had three pet beds for Byrd that he never used. My gaze swung up to find Tim had arrived. One look at Tim eased the last of my worries. The convenience store owner had a smile so wide it crinkled his eyes, telling me the parrot's new home was going to be great for his self-esteem.

I waved Tim over eagerly. "Hi, Tim. Bree is getting Elvis ready to go, and I have a bag for you to take home. Items to help with the transition."

"Thank you so much," the man beamed. "I can't tell you how excited the wife and I are to have him."

Out of the corner of my eye, I saw Bree carry out the cage, the parrot safely inside. As soon as Elvis saw Tim, he flapped his wings and bobbed his head back and forth in a little happy dance.

"Timmy! Timmy! Timmy!" the bird sang.

The man took the cage from Bree, who followed him

out, carrying the care package. As they stepped out, she looked at me over her shoulder and shot a little wink before she closed the door behind them. My chest swelled with emotion as I watched them through the front window. No matter what happened lately, this was what made it all better. Nothing beats seeing a pet get a second chance at a happy home.

"Um, Lia?" Ryder said from down the hallway. "Not to bother you, but you might want to get in here. Benny just started to glow."

I dabbed at the corners of my eyes, brushing away any traces of doubt or fear that threatened to betray my composure. Squaring my shoulders, I summoned every ounce of resolve within me, ready to confront whatever awaited me in the examination room. With a pivot of the heels, I marched down the hallway.

When I'd first opened the clinic, I had no idea what a difference it would make for the town and the paranormals living here. Though it was the difference it had made in me I hadn't anticipated.

Two murders solved.

A glowing hellhound.

Things were never simple at the Sunny Days Clinic, were they? Luckily for everyone involved, complicated was exactly how I liked it.

Opening the door to the room, my jaw hit the floor, my heart dropping to join it a few seconds later.

"Wow," I whispered. "You weren't kidding."

"This is terrible!" the detective said, holding the Frenchie at arm's length.

The room lit up like a beacon from the golden light emanating from the adorable pup.

I chuckled, closing the door behind me. "No," I said, my grin widening. "This is perfection."

ABOUT SEDONA JADE

Sedona Jade is the cozy side of a quirky coin; she channels her sarcasm not only into annoying her husband and children, but also into her characters as they stumble their way through unraveling mysteries. Embracing the charm of the cozy paranormal mystery genre, she spins tales set in small towns brimming with secret magic, peculiar happenings, and where a search in every nook and cranny could yield a clue. Her narratives intertwine the everyday with the supernatural, all laced with a generous helping of humor, sarcasm, and heart.

Away from the writing desk, she indulges in the simplicities of life—hiking, photography, and spending quality time with her family. At home, she's surrounded by a delightful mix of furry friends and an impressive assembly of reptiles, reflecting her love for all creatures great and small... including her belly-rub-loving sidekick, Faux the Arctic Fox!

www.sedonajade.com

ABOUT AMY STAKE

Amy Stake is a cozy mystery connoisseur and lover of all things paranormal. Much like a dragon, she loves collecting —aka hoarding—keyboards and all the pretty notebooks she can get her hands on. Amy is Sedona Jade's partner in paracozy crime... and with these two putting their wit and whimsical senses of humor together, you're guaranteed a wild ride of a story!

www.ingramcontent.com/pod-product-compliance
Lightning Source LLC
Chambersburg PA
CBHW030112180626
46812CB00002B/390